MISTRESS OF SIN

EIGHTY MILLION WHORES!

That was what Kevin Lyle called the women of the world. Eighty million whores, hot and panting for any guy who had what ehy wanted: money, fame, security, or just that quick blind stab of passion. And Kevin Lyle, Hollywood story-editor, knew it was the truth . . . look at his wife: Donna, with her full, lush body who bedded down every time the demand in her grew too great — it didn't matter with whom! Or Audrey, who didn't care what perversion, what horrors were asked of her as long as she became a star. And then there was Lorayne who cried out: "Hurt me! Hurt me!" when Lyle was locked in her arms. Lorayne who allowed herself to be picked up and then made wailing sounds of lust when a man touched her. Whores . . . all of them . . . every one of them . . . but he was tied to them by a chain of passion he could not break. A chain of sin . . .

MISTRESS OF SIN

by
Don Elliott
(Robert Silverberg)

FICTION HOUSE
Adult Book

MISTRESS OF SIN

For more titles in the Fiction House library,
visit our website: **www.FictionHousePress.com**

"Mistress of Sin" was published in 1962. No copyright regis-
tration. This work is Public Domain.

First Fiction House edition January 2021

isbn 978-1-64720-216-3

Published by
Fiction House Press
www.FictionHousePress.com

Chapter One

KEVIN LYLE FIRST MET HER at a stoplight on Wilshire Boulevard a block before it crosses La Cienega. The light turned red when he was three quarters of the way down the block. and he heeled the brake and brought the sleek white convertible to a halt right alongside a bus stop, and there she was.

She stood near the curb, looking at him with frank interest. He looked back. She was about twenty, maybe — there was a youthful fresh-ness. that was for sure. Tight black toreador pants set off the lush fullness of her hips and buttocks. A tucked-in silk shirt glinted with bright sheen over the steep, exciting mounds of her breasts. Her hair was golden, and pulled back tight from the front of her scalp to dangle in a narrow glistening pony-tail behind.

Lyle smiled at her. She smiled back.

"Going my way?" she asked. Her voice was

deep and throaty, a siren's voice.

"Could be. Where you heading?" Lyle asked, grateful for the informality that a top-down convertible provided.

"Downtown. Fourth and Broadway."

"I'll take you right there." Lyle said. "Hop in."

He reached across and pushed the door open for her. She slid into the bucket seat next to him. The light changed, and an impatient Angeleno leaned on his horn behind them. Lyle put the car in motion. His throat felt strangely dry, his heart was moving faster than usual, and his hands gripped the wheel tightly. He risked his life to grab a sideways look at his passenger. Her face had a serene classical beauty in profile, and the contour of her breasts against the tight shirt was so startling as to make him nearly drive up onto the sidewalk.

"I'm not taking you out of your way, am I?" she asked.

"Not a bit. I've got to stop off at my lawyer's for a moment, and his office is on Spring and 6th. So it's just a couple of blocks from where you're heading. Then I'll pick up the freeway and head out to Pasadena to see my wife."

"You say it like you're separated from her," the girl remarked.

"Smart lassie." Lyle smiled bitterly. "We split up two months ago. Nothing permanent yet, just a separation. She's got possession of our house for the moment. And of our children. The bitch." He wondered why he was telling all this to a girl he had known only three minutes.

"How many children do you have?"

"Two. Boy of five, girl of four. There ought to have been a three-year-old, too. We were having them all in a hurry, you see. But the baby died. Hit by a car in January."

"Oh. I'm sorry."

"So was I. My wife was busy with her lover at the time. Couldn't keep her eyes on the kid." Lyle shook his head. "It's too nice a day for such a morbid conversation."

"Yes, it's beautiful today," the girl agreed.

And so are you, Lyle thought. He felt a constricting sensation in his chest. The day was golden, a lilting June Saturday with the temperature in the high 70's and not a trace of smog. And there was this beautiful girl by his side in the car. Lyle's pulse throbbed. He hadn't been having a very active sex life since the separation. Right at the outset there'd been a couple of casual affairs — Los Angeles is full of twitchy-tailed females ready to spread for a ruggedly handsome man of thirty-six with movie connections — but lately, at his lawyer's advice, he'd been living something of a monastic existence. Which wasn't easy for him to do, all things considered. Especially when there was a girl like this next to him in the car. He knew what he wanted to do now. He wanted to turn off Wilshire and head for Elysion Park or anyplace else where there might be trees and a little privacy, take her clothes off, nestle between her thighs and cup the ripe mounds of her bare breasts in his hands.

Instead he said, as they slowed for another red light, "Are you in the movies?"

She laughed. "Kind of."

"Which means?"

"Which means I'm a hopeful. I'm in the movies as far as the front reception desk."

"No luck?"

"Not yet. But I've only been here six months. I haven't given up yet."

"If a girl with your looks can't make it in this town, nobody can," Lyle said. "What's the trouble? Who's your agent?"

"Don't have one," the girl said. "That's part of the trouble."

"You expect to get somewhere on your own?"

"I was with Joe Hammond," she said. "You know him?"

"That lecherous bastard? Sure," Lyle said.

"Lecherous is the word. He was going to make me into the next Jayne Mansfield, he said. All I had to do was be patient, cooperate, and sleep with him."

"So you walked out?"

"Like hell I did." the girl said in a weary, sophisticated voice far older than her twenty years. "I slept with him. It wasn't like I had anything to lose. But he was filthy—I wouldn't want to tell you what be tried to get me to do. He's a real pervert, you know?"

"I've heard rumors," Lyle said. "But you hear a lot of noise around this town."

"Anything you heard about Joe Hammond,

it's true. Well, I wouldn't cooperate. And I made him sore. So sore that when I walked out he promised me I'd never get a movie job in my life, not anywhere, and so far he's been right."

"Joe Hammond can't run a one-man blacklist."

"Then why don't I have a new agent? I can't get anybody reputable to take me on. And you know how it is when you walk in on your own. Don't call us, we'll call you. And similar baloney. Maybe you know. Are you in the movies?"

"Kind of," Lyle said with a wry grin.

"Now it's my turn. What do you mean?" she asked. "You an actor?"

"Nope. Front office."

"You aren't with Casting," she said. "I wouldn't have the luck to hop a ride with a man from Casting."

"Nope, you wouldn't. I'm a story editor. You ever hear of Leo Naumann?"

"Who hasn't?"

"Well. Naumann pays me large sums of money a year to read books, talk to authors, and be wined and dined by literary agents. I pick the books from which Naumann picks the books he's going to film. It's a dull job."

"Why don't you become an actor? You've got the physique for it, and the face, and—"

"And everything but the talent," Lyle said. "Not that you need a hell of a lot to get along in this town. But I don't have the temperament to act, either. And I don't need the money. I've got simple tastes. I can be happy on fifty grand a year. I don't need half a million."

"How long you been doing this kind of work?"

"Seven years. I wrote film scripts before that. You must have seen a lot of my stuff when you were a kid. If you liked cowboy movies and situation comedies and crap like that. But you wouldn't remember the names of any of my films. I can't even remember them myself. For that matter, I don't even know *your* name."

"Lorayne Winant. What's yours?"

"Kevin Lyle."

"That your real name?"

"Oddly enough, it is. You?"

"The Winant's real. But my mother called me Bessie. I figured I'd do better as Lorayne."

"You don't look like a Bessie."

"Thanks, I suppose."

"So you've been trying to get into the movies," Lyle said. "And in the meanwhile?"

"I work in a night club."

"Selling cigarettes? Checking hats?"

"I dance," Lorayne said. "It's sort of a joke. I come out wearing a bunch of rhinestones and I wiggle around for a while, three times a night. It pays a big hundred-twenty a week. Which is why I take buses downtown instead of zooming along in a Mercedes-Benz."

"You may be hurting your chances with a big studio if you work as a stripper," Lyle said.

"I don't strip. I just dance in scanty costumes. Anyway, I got to live. I could be doing worse things for a living."

"I suppose you could."

"They say a lot of funny things about your boss." Loyrane went on. "Any of them true? Like —"

"Skip it," Lyle said quickly. "I don't talk about my employers's private life."

"Big Brother may be watching, huh? You think he's got the windshield wipers bugged?"

"I don't talk about him," Lyle repeated doggedly. "I like my job. Let's change the subject."

"Okay," Lorayne said, pouting. "What are you doing tonight?"

"Huh?"

"You heard me. You obviously aren't going to spend the night with your wife. What are you going to do this evening?"

"Go home and curl up with a bad book."

"On Saturday night?"

"I'm old and weary, girl. I need my rest."

"How about coming to the club where I work? Stop in around midnight and see the last show. Here." She fumbled in her tiny handbag and drew out a printed card, which she stuck in a corner of his dashboard. "Show this card to the manager and he'll let you come backstage to meet me. We can go for a drive or something afterward."

"Well —"

"Or don't you like me?"

Lyle didn't know what the girl was angling at, but he could guess. What she wanted, more than a night in bed with Kevin, was an introduction to Leo Naumann. Lyle moistened his lips. He didn't like being used as a go-between.

But the girl was ravishingly beautiful, and there was that dull ache in him that told of too many lonely nights. Besides, if she was the sort of girl Naumann went for, there would be some advantages for him. Even after seven years with Leo, Lyle had to keep on demonstrating his value every week.

"I'll see," Lyle said. "Depends on what time I get back tonight. Where is the place?"

"The address is on the card. It's on the Sunset Strip. You'll like it."

He turned off Wilshire as it passed under the Harbor Freeway and died into Fifth. Driving past Pershing Square, he let the girl off at Fifth and Broadway.

"See you tonight?" she said hopefully.

"Maybe."

She blew him a kiss and left the car. He watched the way her buttocks tightened against the seat of her pants. She had a nice trim body. He could almost taste desire in his mouth. A muscle throbbed in his cheek as he pictured himself lying atop the blonde girl, his body moving rhythmically, his hands caressing the satiny slopes of her breasts, the silky smoothness of her shoulders.

She was his for the asking. So were plenty of others, but there was something special about this one. She promised more than a couple of sweaty seconds of tingling sensation. She promised excitement.

The light changed, and he swung right toward Spring, gliding the car into the first parking lot he came to. Lyle didn't like downtown Los Angeles. It was hectic and crowded and ugly; the buildings had an old-fashioned sooty drabness about them that reminded him of Philadelphia, of New York, of Cincinnati. The hideous blotch of the downtown area was to the city of palm trees and glistening new buildings as a boiler room is to an ultra-modern ocean liner.

He couldn't understand how his lawyer, Ben Montereale, could stand keeping an office down here. Rents were lower here than in Hollywood or Santa Monica, sure. But Ben didn't need to worry about overhead, not with an income pushing six figures a year just from divorce cases alone. The reason, Lyle thought, was simply that Ben liked squalor. And he liked to drag his high-priced clients downtown for conferences.

The lawyer's office was on the third floor of a towering office building. Lyle rode up. Montereale's secretary admitted him quickly.

Ben Montereale was a short, chunky man of fifty, bald on top, jowly, never without a stub of a cigar in his mouth. He was a native New Yorker, and would always be a New Yorker, even though he had lived in L. A. for twenty years. He glanced up at Lyle owlishly from behind thick glasses and said, "Grab a seat, Kevin. First off, I had a phone call from your wife a couple minutes ago."

"What did the bitch want?"

"She had a message for you. She says she isn't feeling well today, and could you please come to visit the kids tomorrow afternoon instead."

It was like a knife in Lyle's body. "She promised me this visit three weeks ago. I feel like going out there anyway. I'm not going there to visit her. And she can't keep me away legally. I moved out voluntarily."

"Don't go today," Montereale advised quietly. "Don't antagonize her. It won't pay, Kevin. Let her have her way, until, *blamm!* We slap her with everything. Go out there tomorrow instead. You can wait one more day."

"I suppose."

"Okay, now." Montereale riffled papers on his desk. "I been talking with her lawyer. Just preliminary skirmishes, you understand. The way I get it, if you sue on grounds of adultery, she'll file a countersuit alleging everything from adultery to mental cruelty and asking ten billion bucks' alimony. As well as the kids."

"But —"

"Shut up. Just because you caught some guy laying her, that don't mean you've got a case. The court's always on the woman's side. Just how clean are your own hands?"

"Eh?"

Montereale leaned forward and said slowly, as through talking to a child, "Did you ever have carnal knowledge of another woman while you were still living with Donna?"

"Look, Ben —"

"Don't weasel. Level with me or I can't help you. Did you?"

"Yes. Twice."

"What circumstances?"

"Once when Donna was in the hospital having Carolyn. I just got too goddam hot, and some little starlet came along and waved her boobs at me."

"That was, four years ago. Okay. What was the other?"

"Last winter at Cuernavace. Donna and I had a big fight and I went off and had too much tequila and wound up in the sack with a senorita."

"Donna find out about it?"

"She knew I was out all night. I guess she could draw her own conclusions."

Montereale lifted a bushy eyebrow. "Six years of marriage and you only stepped out *twice?* Come off it, Kevin."

"I told you the truth."

"It ain't natural."

"I loved Donna." Lyle said quietly. "I wasn't interested in other women. The starlet four years ago was a fluke. All the rest of the time I got all the loving I needed from Carolyn. Until she began to change. And even then there was just the Mexican girl, until the time I moved out."

"Maybe we got a chance, then," Montereale said. "But I don't know. They can dig up half a dozen of Naumann's starlets who'll swear you laid them nine ways from Sunday. Try and disprove it. Let them just find out about that deal four years ago and they'll be marching every little piece in Southern California through the courtroom as a mistress of yours."

Lyle shook his head. "I don't understand it, Ben. Here I caught my own wife in bed with her lover, and through her negligence one of my children was killed, and still I can't get a divorce and custody of the other two kids, and you say I've got to take the *defensive?*"

"We can't prove the baby was killed while Donna was entertaining her lover, you know. And she's prepared to fight tooth and nail for the kids. I'm just warning you. From here on in she'll be out to besmirch your character so she can get custody. Wouldn't surprise me if she had a detective slapped on you."

"She wouldn't!"

"Wanta bet? That's why I said keep away from the women. Don't mess around till this is settled."

"It could take months, Ben! I'm no goddam celibate!"

"You want those kids?"

"Of course. But —"

"But nothing. For the next few months, you pretend you never heard of sex. If you get the itch real bad, well, you remember what you used to do when you were fifteen and didn't have a handy girl around —"

Lyle stared bleakly at the lawyer. "I haven't had a woman in more than a month, Ben. I'm going nuts. The court won't hold it against me. I'm a healthy man with normal instincts, that's all. They don't expect me —"

"They expect you to be a saint. You practically have to be, before the court will take kids away from their mother. Another thing. When visiting Donna. She might just try to get you to go to bed with her. Don't do it. It'll be a trap to prove that you're morally unfit to get the kids."

"I wouldn't sleep with Donna again if —"

Montereale shook his head. "You just told me you're itching. Donna's a lovely woman. Suppose you drive out there tomorrow and when you're through visiting the kids she takes you into the bedroom and unzips her dress and starts fooling around with you? And talking about a reconciliation, maybe, while she does it? What are you going to do? Five to one says you'll want to climb on top of her."

Lyle was silent. He knew Montereale was right.

The lawyer went on, "Well, just don't do it. You don't want any reconciliations. and neither does she. All you both want is the kids, and she'll try every trick in the book to get them. So you just watch out." In a different voice Montereale said, "Look, Kevin, if you gotta have a woman, for Christ's sake be *careful* about it. Okay?"

"Okay, Ben."

"That's it. I'll phone you if anything happens."

"Sure thing, Ben." Lyle rose. "Thanks for everything."

"Don't mention it. How's your boss coming along?"

"Leo? Doing just fine. The gross on *Edge of Eternity* will knock your eye out."

"I bet. What I mean is, you think Leo's going to have some business for me soon? A paternity suit, or another one of those perversion things that's got to be hushed up?"

Lyle's face went bleak. "You ought to know better than to joke about Leo, Ben."

"Yeah. I guess so. That guy really gets me, though. I don't see how you can stand working for him."

"His dough is as green as the next guy's, Ben. I don't give a damn about his private life so long as his checks get through the bank."

Montereale shrugged. "I suppose. Take it slow, man. And don't worry. Old Benny'll see you through this thing okay. If you don't foul him up."

"I'll try not to, Ben. So long."

CHAPTER TWO

OUTSIDE THE LAWYERS'S OFFICE, standing in the street, Lyle felt a deep sense of despair. So Donna would fight for the kids? She didn't deserve them, of course, but that didn't matter; it would be a messy custody battle, and everybody would come out of it the loser, the children worst of all. Lyle knew what Donna was really after. She wanted him to call off his adultery suit, let her divorce him on the standard mental cruelty bit, and divide property and kids fifty-fifty, with him paying her a fat pile of dough and getting custody of the kids only six months out of the year. If he planned to raise a stink, she would raise a counter-stink. It might very well cost him his job. Leo Naumann had a horror of bad publicity. If anyone around the Naumann office was going to be a sinner, it was going to be L. N. himself and none of the underlings. The old man was such a lecherous skunk himself that everyone around him had to be simon-pure to cover up.

Lyle walked up to the parking lot. It was only one in the afternoon, now. He had been figuring on getting to Donna's by quarter to two, staying there till five or six to play with the kids, then leaving, treating himself to dinner someplace decent, and getting home around eight or nine. He had a book to read, galley proofs of a novel about emerging Africa that Naumann was thinking of making into his next blockbuster.

Everybody was trying to make timely films about Africa now, and this was going to be a smash best seller, so Naumann wanted an opinion on it in a hurry. Lyle might just as well have said without reading it, "Buy it," because he knew it was headed for big money, but he didn't work that way. Leo trusted him to *read* the damned books, and Lyle read them.

Now there was a whole afternoon empty, though. A thought occurred. *Suppose I go home and read the book now. I can get halfway through it by nine or ten o'clock, and then I can go over to the Strip and take in that nightclub —*

He cut the thought off, frowning. That was smart, he told himself. Real smart. Have a conference with your lawyer, have him warn you to stay clear of bedroom complications, and then start thinking about making dates with ambitious starlets two minutes after you leave his office.

But the girl magnetized him.

He wanted her.

Lyle shrugged and got his car out of the parking lot. As he threaded his way back toward Wilshire, he went over the details of his conversation with Montereale. He wasn't surprised that Donna was planning to fight him; Donna had turned into a cold calculating bitch, and she was totally unscrupulous when it came to getting what she wanted. It hadn't occurred to Lyle that Donna might try to seduce him. But it was just the sort of trick she would try — and then claim that he had compelled her to have intercourse with him against her will. It always looked bad when a separated couple tore off a quick one that way.

Fidgeting, Lyle admitted that in his present state of nerves he'd easily fall victim to Donna's wiles if she tried to pull something like that. Donna was a full-bodied, almost voluptuous woman, and he was hard up. He could be tempted by her. *Maybe I better be prepared*, he thought. *Like by getting something tonight, just to take the edge off my nerves before I see her tomorrow —*

He headed up Wilshire, past General MacArthur Park, past the glossy bank buildings and hotels, past Normandie Avenue and La Brea and Fairfax. Since moving out of his place in Pasadena, he had rented a two-room hotel suite at a small residential hotel just north of Wilshire, a ten-minute drive from Leo Naumann's Beverly Hills home and a half-hour drive from Naumann's main office in Culver City. For $50 a week he had modern furniture, peace and quiet, and a fairly central location. He took all his meals out.

Parking the car out front, Lyle rode upstairs to his fifth-floor suite and let himself in. A stack of mail stood on the table just within the door, most of it bills that Donna had forwarded. When he had moved out, he had told her to send any bills on her personal expenses up till that day to him, and all involving household expenses for the kids. So she sent them. Once or twice she tried to slip in an extra on him, like the dentist bill to have her teeth cleaned, dated a month after he had moved out. He didn't pay those. He just made notations of them, and sent them back telling her to wait till after the divorce settlement for stuff like that.

He kicked off his shoes and sprawled out on the couch with the book he was to read this weekend. A dozen other waited for him. Everybody in the world wanted Leo Naumann to make a film out of his book, and small wonder; Naumann's films had astonishing grosses, all over the world. The man was morally corrupt, but he had a sure instinct for pleasing an audience all the way from the critical intellectuals to the popcorn set. Naumann only went after the bestsellers, the talked-about books. He liked to make movies that would be timely and timeless at the same time. An independent producer, Naumann did his own directing as well. Banks fell all over themselves in their hurry to lend him money.

Lyle opened the book. Galley proofs, of

course; Naumann never needed to wait long to read a book when galleys were available. Eight hundred sixty-seven pages, this one was, on heavy shiny sheets bound together by spiralling rings of plastic. The book was the size of a telephone directory, and twice as heavy. Lyle opened it to the first page and began to read.

It was one of those panoramic things, a novel set in a mythical Central African country just coming to independence. It began in A. D. 1400 with the story of a tribal emperor, and then, with half a million characters and two dozen interlocking plots, moved tortuously upward through the era of slave raiders to that of imperialism to the present time and independence. A literal film of the whole book would run a hundred reels. What Leo would do, Lyle thought, would be to carve the central section out — the romance of a messianic African political leader and a wealthy white woman of liberal tendencies — and film that, making the movie into a miscegenation shocker with a political background. Some poor bastard would be paid $5000 a week to shape the unwieldy mass into a script that would offend neither the most diehard segregationist nor the NAACP, and Leo Naumann would drag off a few more Oscars for his already impressive shelf.

Lyle slogged steadily through the book at a rate of better than a page a minute, taking notes as he went. By seven o'clock, he was well past the halfway point, and ferociously hungry. He went down to the hotel restaurant, polished off a sirloin steak and three bottles of Danish beer, and returned to his suite. He began to step up his reading pace. At ten minutes after ten that evening he turned over the eight hundred sixty-seventh page, closed the cardboard binding, and went to the phone to call Leo Naumann.

A girl answered — Leo's current playmate, Lyle figured. A moment later Naumann came to the phone. Lyle was willing to bet that the movie magnate was stark naked and getting a rubdown while he spoke.

"What is it, Kevin?"

"I finished the Africa book, Leo." Everyone called Naumann by his first name. It was part of the phony nice-guy atmosphere he tried to cultivate.

"What's the report?"

"Double plus," Llye said. "There's a hell of a movie in that book, Leo. You'll have another smash. This one's got real scope, color — no pun — and drama. Film it on location somewhere in Ghana or the Congo. It can't miss."

"Okay. Buy it," Naumann said.

Lyle blinked. "After you've read it, of course."

"No, buy it right now. I'll read it on Monday. If you say it can't miss, it can't miss."

Lyle began to sweat. Naumann almost always insisted on reading books himself before he confirmed Lyle's opinion; a couple of times he had vetoed a Lyle choice. Lyle didn't want to take the responsibility for the purchase. But obviously Naumann was busy with some cutie this weekend and didn't have time to read the book, yet didn't want it to slip through his fingers.

"It's too late to phone New York tonight," Lyle began hesitantly.

"The hell it is. What time is it?"

"After ten."

"So it's one in the morning in New York. On Saturday night that's too late? Who's the agent?"

"Byrce."

"Okay, you tell Bryce right now," Naumann ordered. "Tell the operator to keep trying till you get him. Offer a hundred grand for the book. If Bryce sounds doubtful, raise him fifty grand. Don't go above half million. If Bryce likes the sound of the dough, tell him to hop a plane Monday morning and come out here to talk contract."

"Right. I'll phone you back when I know."

There was a click. Lyle put down the dead phone, then dialed Long Distance.

Buying a book was a complicated process. The first thing was to get hold of the agent and tell him how much Naumann was willing to pay. Then agent and producer and a dozen lawyers got together and worked out the contract in such a way as to let a nominal number of dollars fall into Uncle Sam's hands. Lyle's job ended once he got an agent to agree to negotiate.

Naumann always threw big money around. Half the time he could get a book for twenty grand instead of half a million, but he preferrred the big splash. It was better publicity, paid off better in the long run. You didn't gross fifteen million bucks on a film made from a bargain book. You had to think big if you wanted big results.

The agent had a Park Avenue apartment. He was home, luckily for Lyle, giving a party. He came to the phone in a hurry when he heard who was calling.

"Yes, Mr. Lyle!"

"Mr. Naumann is interested in the novel," Lyle said.

"Glad to hear that. Of course, we've already had several offers —"

"Naumann wants the book." Lyle felt reckless, now that he was this far out on the limb. "How does a hundred thousand sound, Bryce?"

"Well, to be frank —"

"To be frank, you've been offered more. Okay," Lyle said. "You want to get back to your party, and I've got some things to do too. What sort of cash are you interested in?"

"Call it three hundred thousand, Mr. Lyle. Plus a small piece of the gross, of course."

"I think we'll be able to arrange that," Lyle said. "Can you come to Mr. Naumann's office by Monday afternoon for the signing?"

"I'm on my way first thing Monday Ayem," Bryce said.

Lyle was grinning as he put down the phone. The ten-percenter had been practically beside himself with glee at the idea of selling his book to Naumann, much as he had tried to hide the fact. Lyle felt weary. The transaction had bored him. A few minutes of expensive phone conversation, a few hundred thousand dollars of someone else's money, and a new blockbuster was on its way. Let Bryce and Naumann haggle about the actual details. A rough agreement had been reached, and that was enough to complete Lyle's end of the deal.

He phoned Naumann back, told him the outcome. Business was now out of the way. He could relax.

He fished the card out of his wallet. The Club Orientale, it was called. At half past ten. Lyle thought of that visit with the kids tomorrow. And Donna.

He needed his nerves strengthened. To hell with Montereale's advice about staying away from women. It was a lot more risky for him to get seduced by his own wife than to go to bed with a swivel-hipped blond broad. He went downstairs, got into his car, began to drive. The streets flowed by, and then he found himself on the garishly bright Sunset Strip, and a neon blinker up ahead advertised the proximity of the Club Orientale.

A functionary in pasha's turban and full beard parked his car for him. Lyle went inside.

The place had an oriental angle, all right, only the decorator had probably had an advanced case of schizophrenia. There were Japanese lanterns, Chinese gongs, Turkish ornaments, a weird mishmash of what was considered eastern motif. Lyle let himself be led down front, to a tiny table. The place was dark; most of the people there were handholding couples in their twenties and thirties, doing a lot of busy drinking.

A waiter took his order. Lyle asked for bourbon. Then he waited.

He had used up four bucks' worth of bourbon by the time the show started, at midnight. It was the usual nightclub routine, a wisecracking comic and a couple of sword dancers and a stripper who did a bare-breasted hootcykootch. The act was pretty tasteful, though. Not a flesh act at all, except in spots. When Lorayne came out for the first time. she was with four other girls, all of them wearing tight sheaths glittering with spangles. He had eyes only for her. The sheath molded her full breasts, letting creamy globes half spill over the top. It clung skintight down to her abdomen, where it came to an abrupt ending. Her long legs fulfilled the promise of the toreador pants.

The girls danced, or rather moved rhythmically, with a lot of hip and bosom action. Once Lorayne seemed to catch sight of him, and she winked. Desire lanced through him.

She danced off. Lyle relaxed again.

She came on later. This time she was alone, and she was wearing just a G-string and a tiny bra. It barely covered her nipples. It was a harness affair, held on ingeniously. It glittered with rhinestones. She did her solo dance, undulating skilfully. The G-string left the globes of her buttocks nearly bare, just hiding the crucial area. Lyle sweated. She was a magnificent animal, constructed for making love.

She shuffled off, to big applause. The comic returned to do the finale of the show. Lyle rose from his seat and made his way through the near-darkness to the side door. He showed his card to the head waiter.

"Miss Winant asked me to meet her back-stage," Lyle whispered.

The waiter looked at the card, nodded, and pointed to the passageway. "Back there. You'll find her."

"Thanks," Lyle said, slipping the man a five.

He headed into the corridor. The backstage area was narrow and lined with small cubicles. Showgirls in various stages of undress wan-dered back and forth. Lyle almost bumped into one girl who was wearing only underpants, and all he said was, "Excuse me." The blonde's full, bouncing breasts didn't interest him now. He was singlemindedly focussed on another blonde named Lorayne.

He found a dressingroom that bore a sticker saying, MISS WINANT. Voices were coming from within.

"Don't be like that, honey. Gimme a kiss." It was a deep masculine voice, thick with liquor.

"I told you to get out of here, Nick, and I meant it," Lorayne said sharply. "You don't have any business back here. You could get thrown out."

"I do so have business. With you."

"Get your filthy hands off me!"

Lyle pulled the dressingroom door open

25

without knocking. He saw a man in his late thirties, tall and goodlooking — an actor, maybe. He was wearing evening clothes, and he had fine, even features, cleancut, a little too regular. He had his hand clasped tightly around Lorayne's wrist.

She was wearing nothing but her G-string. Her breasts were exposed and there were red scuffmarks along the side of one breast that showed how her bra had been ripped away. She was struggling. Her breasts were magnificent, firm rounded snowy hills tipped with red. Her eyes gleamed with relief as she caught sight of Lyle.

"This drunk bothering you?" Lyle asked.

"Get him out of here, will you? He thinks he owns me, just because I was nice to him a couple of times —"

"A couple of times?" roared the drunk. "I've laid you more often than I can count, and —"

"Get him out of here," Lorayne said.

"You heard her," Lyle snapped, feeling uneasy about butting into this. "Out."

"Who the hell are you?"

The answer was a fist. It glanced off the side of Lyle's cheek, snapping his head back with a nasty crack. Lyle straightened around. He felt a touch of panic. This would look fine in the papers, Lyle thought, if he got arrested for brawling in a dancer's dressing-room. The divorce court would really love it.

But now that he was involved, there was no turning back. Rage flowed through him. The drunk was weaving unsteadily.

Lyle stepped forward. He was a little bigger than the other, and a lot heavier. His fist climbed upward, connecting solidly with the other's jaw. Lyle felt the impact and saw a trickle of blood sprouting from the other's cut lip.

"Let him have it!" Lorayne was squealing excitedly. "Let him have it hard!"

The drunk didn't seem to know what was going on. He landed one good punch that bruised Lyle's upper lip and cut it slightly. But that was the last solid hit he scored. Lyle waded in, fists swinging in a way they hadn't done since he was a kid. He pounded a right and a left into the drunk's chest just above the heart, followed with another right into the stomach. The drunk gagged.

Lyle hit him in the face and a fountain of blood spurted from that neat, straight nose. Another punch cauliflowered an ear and nearly sent the drunk spinning to the ground. He was holding up his hands in protest, trying dimly to ward off Lyle's blows. But Lyle was warming to the fight, getting all the frustrations and bitteriness of the last two months out of his system in violent catharsis. He rained punches down on the defenseless drunk. The tuxedo became splattered with red. Once, Lyle saw the girl's face — eyes bright with pleasure as she watched each punch. She wasn't bothering to cover her bare breasts, either.

Finally the other dropped to his knees. His

face was a bloody mess. Lyle picked the man up by his collar, shoved him to the door of the tiny dressingroom, and heaved him out into the corridor. He sprawled out on the floor, vomiting out his night's liquor.

Lyle shut the door and slid the bolt. Lorayne was smiling at him, and her naked breasts rose excitedly like twin grapefruits. They were big breasts, but high, and unmarred by veins. The nipples were small, dark red, set in flawlessly rounded aureoles. Little beads of sweat from the closeness in the room and her own recent exertions glistened on her breasts. Her body was marvelous, narrowing at the waist, then widening sensuously at the hips.

Lyle's hands stung, and his knuckles were covered with blood. There was blood on his face, too, from the split lip he had sustained. Lorayne came forward.

"You were wonderful," she breathed. "That pest has been hanging around here for days, bothering me."

"Who is he?"

"An actor. Or an ex-actor. He's been out of work for two years. Everyone hates him. He started following me around, gave me a line about introducing me to his agent. That was before I found out how lousy his agent is. But I couldn't get rid of the guy."

"I don't think he'll come back after tonight," Lyle said, grinning. "I sort of went a little wild when I saw him in here pawing you."

"I'm so glad you came. Did you visit your

wife?"

"No. She postponed it till tomorrow."

"I'm sorry. But —"

The magnetism of her practically nude body cut off further conversation. Lyle drew her close to him, and she slipped her arms around his body. Her breasts and thighs ground against his body. She took his hands in hers, lifted them to her lips, and kissed them. She seemed to enjoy the taste! And then she put her lips to Lyle's, gently, her tongue covering his cut and seeming to sip his blood. Suddenly the tongue darted into his mouth. She began to pant and grind furiously against him. His hands stroked her back, then slipped between their tightly pressed bodies to cup the fullness of her breasts. The two firm globes of flesh were warm and vital in his hands. The nipples, hard with passion, pressed against his palms. He felt desire making him go rigid.

A tremendous feeling of excitement coursed through him. The fight had keyed him up. He wasn't a man who liked violence, but the jolt of adrenalin his system had received was taking its effect, stimulating him. He hardly noticed the fierce pain as her mouth pressed tight against his bruised lips. His hand groped for the G-string that was her sole garment. He had trouble getting it open.

"No — you'll rip it," she murmured.

Deftly, she peeled it away. She was naked, now, and he ran his hands down the firmness of her buttocks, feeling the taut flesh, the gentle dimples, the silkiness of her skin. She began to pant, and then a moment later she was stripping him, peeling away his clothes and tossing them into the corner of the dressing-room . . . .

He had her for the first time right there, animallike, on the cold stone floor of the small dressingroom. The moment their bodies were joined she began to writhe and whimper in delight. He arched his body up from hers, looking down, seeing her gleaming with sweat, her breasts rising and falling rapidly, her face red where the blood from his cut had dripped on it. He plunged, driving himself deeper within her, and she gasped and moaned and clawed at him and locked her muscular thighs tight around him, and he moved deeper and deeper into the soft warmths and heard her long gasp of pleasure, and then he clamped his eyes tight shut and his body shook with the explosion of ecstasy, and it ended.

CHAPTER THREE

SHAKY AND WOBBLY FROM THE reaction to such powerful physical release after so many weeks of abstinence, Lyle separated from her and stood up.

Lorayne remained on the floor, her breath slowly subsiding, her face flushed and excited. After a moment she propped herself on her elbows and looked at him.

"Aren't you glad you decided not to go through that red light on Wilshire this afternoon?" she asked.

"Sure. I hate getting speeding tickets."

"Funny man. Give me a hand."

He hauled her to her feet, and they stood facing each other, a few feet apart, both of them naked in the cramped, moist-aired dressing-room. Lyle's back stung, as did the backs of his arms. He realized she had scratched him at the height of her ecstasy. And bitten his shoulder. *What a wildcat*, he thought.

Even now, she looked tensed, ready to spring, ready to pull him down to the floor for another round. For all her lush femininity, she had a wiry strength about her that surprised him. He was willing to bet she could outrun him in a hundred-yard dash.

"Was that your last show?" he asked, as he began to gather his clothes.

"Yes." She took a towel from a rack and began to pat the perspiration on her breasts and arms. "I'm free to go home now. Unless you want to stay out for a while."

"I wouldn't mind." There was a gulf of silence between them for a long moment. Lyle knew why the situation had become so awkward. They were two people who had been perfect strangers half a day ago, and now they had been as intimate as two human beings can ever be, and they still didn't know much more about each other than their names. And the savagery of the encounter still troubled him. The fierceness with which he had trounced the drunken pest, and then the wild animal-like way they had taken each other on the floor, blood mixing with sweat. She had clawed and scratched and clung and moaned, more a jungle cat than a woman once their bodies were joined. And now it was time to be civilized again.

Lyle pulled his belt tight. Lorayne hadn't begun to dress yet. She had put down the towel and was moving around the small room, tidying it up, removing the evidences of their passion. Picking up an overturned chair, straightening a table. Lyle watched her. The trim smooth curve of her buttocks was so appealing the thought startled him. She had golden-brown skin, with creamy undertones; she had been out in the sun, but she hadn't tanned really deeply. And the tan was even; no white strips over her breasts and loins.

"I'll wait outside," he suggesteed. "There isn't enough room in here for both of us. Or enough air."

She nodded. "I'll only be a minute, Kevin. Meet me at the bar."

He went out. The drunk had been removed, he noticed, and someone had cleaned up the mess. Only a spot of blood on the white beaver-board partition that served as a wall, and a fugitive odor still lingered on. The backstage area was quiet now. Most of the showgirls were gone. The club would be open for another four or five hours, but only for dancing and drinking; there was no Late Late Show here, it seemed. Lyle made his way through the darkened dance floor and over to the bar.

"Bourbon." he said.

His mouth hurt as the whiskey stung his cut. He had tidied himself up in the dressing-room, and just to look at him there was no way to tell he'd been in a fight. But the tiny nick in his lip throbbed, and his body ached in the places where long-unused muscles had been called into action.

He was finished with his drink and into a second one by the time Lorayne joined him. She was dressed as he had seen her at the bus stop, in the tight pants and silk shirt, with her gleaming pony-tail dangling, down behind. Cat-like, she slid into the seat next to him and said, "Tony, let me have a gimlet, like a dear."

"One gimlet coming up," the bartender said. He began to mix the drink. Lyle sipped his bourbon thoughtfully, wondering what would happen if Ben Montereale walked in right now and found him buying Lorayne a drink. Not that there was much chance of that. Ace divorce lawyer Montereale was a family man with six kids, and on Saturday nights he stayed home in the bosom of his family. But Ben would blow his stack, Lyle thought, if he walked in now. *To hell with him. Man's got a right to have some fun once in a while.* He put his hand on Lorayne's thigh. He realized he was getting a little drunk.

They finished their drinks; Lorayne said goodnight to the bartender, and she and Lyle went outside. The bearded pasha in the parking lot brought Lyle's convertible, and Lyle gave him a dollar.

"Where to?" Lyle asked, getting behind the wheel.

"Let's just drive," Lorayne said. "And fasten that safety-belt, darling. It's messy getting tossed out of an open convertible."

"Never had an accident in my life."

"You never got married in your life till it happened," she said.

"You're so right." He fumbled with the gear-shift and got the car started, jerkily and with a grinding of gears. The road felt a little rough to him, even though he knew it was the same old asphalt as ever. But he felt relaxed and calm. It was a switch to get the loving out of the way *before* going out with a girl. It took some of the uncertainies out of the evening.

He didn't want to risk freeway driving in his present state of befuddlement. Instead, sticking to residential streets, he threaded a rambling path generally northward past Bel Air into the canyon country. He drove for close to an hour, into progressively wilder areas with the sprawling haciendas farther and farther apart. He was getting soberer and soberer all the time. It was close to two in the morning when he suddenly grew weary of driving and turned the car off the road into a dark, secluded scrub forest of twisted junipers and pulled up the handbrake.

"Here we be in the wilderness," he said. "Let's get out and stretch our legs."

They unbelted and stepped out. The place was lonely, with birds hooting overhead and a sliver of moonlight to cast eerie shapes. They walked to the edge of the hill and looked down into dark nothingness for a while. Then they returned to the car and sat down on the dry ground, leaning against the wheels.

Lorayne said, "Are you a native Californian. Kevin?"

"There are only twelve native Californians past the age of thirty," Lyle said. "I'm not one of them. I'm from the suburbs of New York. County of Westchester. Ever hear of it?"

"Sure. Scarsdale, Larchmont, Yonkers, White Plains—"

"You sound like you know the place."

"Only from what I've heard. People are rich there."

"Some of them are. Some aren't."

"What about your family?" she asked.

"Rich. Big mansion in Scarsdale. My father used to have a radio repair shop in the Twenties. Now it's an electronics company with a thousand employees. I own a hundred shares of the stock. He owns a hundred thousand."

"It must be cozy coming from a rich family," Lorayne said. "It takes some of the complications out of life."

"Puts new ones in. I haven't heard a word from my family in seven years. Not since I married Donna. They opposed the match. Said she wasn't the right sort for me." He chuckled bitterly. "The one goddam time in my life that my parents really did know better. But I wouldn't listen."

"Why didn't they like her? Wrong religion or something?"

"Right religion. High church Episcopalian, just like me. Real aristocratic. No, they just didn't like her personality. I told them they were crazy, and I married her anyway, and we all lived to regret it. She was divorced, you see. They didn't want me to marry a divorced woman. Well, now she's got two scalps in her belt."

Lorayne's hand slid up his arm, tightened on

his bicep. He stared off into the darkness. "She used to be married to some actor," he said. "I forget his name. They were married three months and it broke up. The way Donna told it, it was all his fault. But now I'm not so sure." He put his arm around her. It was chilly, up here in these hills. "I was twenty-nine when I got married. Not exactly a spring chicken. I went into it with my eyes open. And I was making thirty thousand a year writing movie scripts. Until Leo Naumann decided to pay me fifty thousand to read books instead."

"Is that what you make?" Lorayne asked, awed. "Fifty thousand?"

"More or less. Minus taxes. Plus bonuses."

"Naumann must be very generous with his money."

"He gets his money's worth," Lyle said. "He doesn't mind calling me up at four in the morning to tell me his brainstorms. And he expects me to function like an IBM thinking machine all hours of the day or night."

"Kevin?"

"What is it, honey?"

"You're going to think I'm a climber, but — but —"

"But you want me to introduce you to Leo Naumann?" he supplied, when she hesitated.

"Yes," she whispered. "I don't see the sense of hiding the truth. I want to get into the movies. More than anything else in the world. And —"

"If you want to get anywhere with Leo Naumann, you'll have to sleep with him," Lyle said.

"I'd do it if it meant a contract. Another roll in the hay more or less won't matter."

"I thought you quit Joe Hammond because he got frisky with you."

"I told you, I'd have slept with him. But he wanted to do disgusting things. With other people, too."

Lyle nodded. He had heard plenty about Joe Hammond's sex habits. Hollywood was like a goldfish bowl, that way. And gossip had it that the hardbitten agent liked his sex peculiar. Odd combinations of two men and a woman, two girls and a man, things like that. And he liked to make love in strange ways, too. The ordinary way wasn't interesting enough for him.

After a long pause Lyle said, "I'll introduce you to Naumann if that's what you want. But I warn you that Leo likes to do odd things too."

"What sort of things?"

He wrestled with himself, knowing it was risky to talk about his boss this way. "One of the things is that he likes little girls." Lyle said finally. "Thirteen, fourteen years old. That shouldn't concern you. But it's the sort of man he is. You know the girl who played the younger daughter in *Edge of Eternity?*"

"Nancy Ryan?"

"That's the one. Leo went wild over her."

"But she's only fourteen, Kevin! My god, she —"

"She was thirteen when Naumann raped her. Now she's got a seven-year contract, half a mil-

38

lion bucks in the bank, and a broken cherry. Pardon the French." He put his hand to his forehead. He realized he must be drunker than he thought, to be telling things like this to a virtual stranger. Naumann would crucify him if a word of this leaked out.

He went on, "Naumann likes to hurt people. He pulls wings off flies in his spare time. He rapes little girls. He rapes big girls, too. And does other things. You ought to see his collection of whips."

"You're kidding."

"I wish I was. But I'll introduce you to him, Lorayne. And you can be the seven thousandth Leo Naumann bed-partner. And if you give him a real good time, he'll make you into a star. A super-star. Interested?"

"I'd — like to meet him, Kevin. All the same."

"Okay. I'll make the sacrifice."

"But I'll go on seeing you," she murmured. "Even if — if Naumann likes me."

"Don't be silly. I don't mess with Naumann's women. If you go to him, our relationship becomes strictly business. I shouldn't be seeing you anyway. My lawyer wants me to live like a hermit till the divorce is worked out."

"You don't have the temperament to live like a hermit." Lorayne said.

"I'm afraid you're right," he agreed.

And then, as though pulled from above by an unseen puppet master, they turned toward each other in the same moment, and his mouth went to hers, and his tongue speared between her lips and deep into her mouth, and her hand caressed him with a touch of fire. He started to gasp as desire abruptly was rekindled in him. They spun around, and she went down on her back, unzipping her pants as she rolled over. He seized them at the knees and dragged them down over her body, though the pants were so tight it was like trying to peel her skin off. At last they came. She had no panties on under‐neath. He stared down at the softness of her thighs, and she pulled her blouse off, unhooked her bra, and lay on the ground naked, waiting for him.

"Let me get the blanket out of the trunk," he said. "You'll get all scratched up lying on those twigs."

"I like getting scratched," she whispered throatily. Sitting up, she threw her arms around his knee and toppled him. He landed on her, and she began to pull off his clothes.

Their lovemaking was as it had been before, only, if anything, more violent. He was aston‐ished by the fury of her responses. She rammed her body against his, imprisoning him within her, then locked her legs around him, crossing her ankles over his back in such a way as to make them one entity instead of two. Then, panting and gasping, they began to roll over the ground like two wild animals coupling in the woods. The ground was cold and hard, and it was covered with dry fallen twigs that crunched beneath their weight. Lyle felt the twigs scratching him. and knew that her more tender skin must be suffering the brunt of it, but she didn't seem to mind. Her mouth fastened on his, his lips within the circle of her small, sharp teeth, and she bit down until he thought she would draw blood.

He caught the frenzied excitement of it. Getting his hands between their bodies, he caught hold of her breasts, palming the full rounded globes of flesh and trapping the stiff upright nipples between his fingers. He squeezed hard, feeling the resilient flesh give.

"Oh, yes, darling, yes," she murmured. "That's it . . . . squeeze them harder . . . . hurt me! Hurt me!"

He gripped her breasts until his fingers began to tremble with the strain. She never ceased the motion of her hips. thrusting her tongue deep within his mouth as she did so. Over and over and over they rolled, and soon she began to tremble and then to jerk convulsively with spasms of pleasure; the spasms passed, and he felt himself reaching culmination. Then he felt the soft warmth of her spasming once again in a second outburst of ecstasy, and he let go all his control and stretched his legs out straight and thrust down deep into her and felt the half-dozen body-rocking bursts of his release.

The savagery of the bout left him exhausted. She went limp beneath him, and he drooped out on top of her, his face between her breasts, his hands still toying with the taut little nipples. He listened to the tattoo of drumbeats that his heart was making, and to the answering booms of her own. Gradually their hearts returned to normal. She ran her hand down his back, stroking the places where ten minutes before her nails had been digging in deep.

He dozed for a while. Then he woke, suddenly, startled to find himself lying naked out here in the cold woods with a naked girl beside him. He sat up. She was smiling at him.

"How do you feel?" she asked.

"Fine."

"So do I. It's been a great night, Kevin."

"One for the books," he said. "Christ, loving you is like loving a jaguar. I've been a married man too long. I've forgotten what it's like really to kick over the traces and let yourself go."

He helped her to her feet. They were both dirty and covered with dead leaves and pieces of wood. He brushed her off, rubbing his hands lovingly over the stunning contours of her breasts and thighs and buttocks. Then she pulled the twigs and leaves off him. They dressed in silence. Their clothes had been scattered over a wide circle: indeed, they had finished up their lovemaking more than twenty feet from where it had begun.

On the way down the hill, Lyle asked, "Where do you live?"

"Hotel in town. Around two blocks from where you picked me up this afternoon."

"Live alone?"

"Yep." She crossed her legs and leaned back. "I tried living with a roommate when I first came here. It didn't work out."

"Where'd you live before you came here?" he asked.

"Oakland. I'm a California girl. I went to college up in Berkeley."

Somehow the thought of this girl sitting in a college classroom diligently taking notes struck him as grotesque. "What did you study?" he asked.

"I was supposed to be a drama major," she said. "I quit after two years. I figured I could do better for myself just going to Hollywood and getting a movie job."

"It isn't as simple as all that."

"So I found out."

"How old are you?" he asked, abruptly.

"Going on twenty-one. In August."

"You're so goddam young. Fifteen years younger than me."

"It isn't so much, really."

"It's a hell of a lot."

"I guess you may be right," she said. "Fifteen years. If you were the precocious type you were laying the girl next door the day I was born."

"I didn't know the difference between men and women till I was twenty-one," Lyle said. "It wasn't till I was thirty that I found out why girls have two big bumps in their sweaters. And tonight was the first time I ever touched a naked woman."

"You fathered your children by remote control, eh?"

"For all I know, I might have," he said, and

what had been a flippant conversation suddenly turned into dead seriousness. The heavy shaft of agony crashed against his heart. He jammed down on the gas pedal bitterly. "No," he said. "That isn't so. Donna's a bitch, and she may have been cheating me from the word go, but the kids are mine. I can see that just by looking in their faces."

"You really love those kids, don't you?" Loryne asked.

"They're the only things I do love in this whole fouled-up world. They aren't old enough to be corrupt yet. If I could only keep them the way they are now. But I can't. Nobody can. Sooner or later the poison gets to everybody, and they begin looking for the dollar. A nation full of whores. A hundred eighty million whores."

"That isn't true, Kevin." Lorayne said. "There are some dedicated people. What about doctors, and researchers, and — and — oh, you're just being cynical. The world will look better to you when this divorce thing is over."

"It couldn't look much worse," he said. He clamped his lips tight together and kicked the speed up to seventy.

An hour later, they were on Wilshire, heading east. He turned off at the street Lorayne indicated, and pulled up in front of her place.

"Want to come upstairs?" she asked.

He shook his head. "I want to, but I won't. I've got to get some sleep some time tonight if I'm going to face my wife tomorrow. And my kids."

She smiled. "Okay. Sleep tight. Will I hear from you tomorrow when you get back?"

"What time do you go to the club?"

"No show on Sunday. I'll be around at home." She opened her purse, gave him a little en-graved card with her name and phone number on it. "Here. You call me. I won't call you."

"That's a switch."

"Isn't it, though," she said. She came close to him, kissed him tenderly, then turned and went into the building. He drove away, back down to Wilshire and over to his hotel. The first gray streaks of dawn were in the sky. He felt bone tired, and he was beginning to get sore from his fist-fight, and his body stung from the places where Lorayne's nails or teeth or the twigs had scratched and scraped him during their bout of love. He hadn't been this tired in years, he thought. Not since he stayed up four nights running to meet a Leo Naumann deadline on a script.

Leo Naumann. He wondered. Lorayne had been quite frank about wanting an introduction. And Leo would really go for a tigress like Lorayne. Leo would be grateful, and Lorayne would become a star, and everyone would be happy.

Except me, Lyle thought. *I get left out. Dammit, I want her for myself! Why should I be Leo Naumann's pimp?*

He let himself into his suite, pulled off his clothes, dropped them on a chair, and flopped down on his narrow bed. He was asleep almost as soon as he had closed his eyes.

CHAPTER FOUR

H E CAME UP OUT OF SLEEP slowly, reluctantly. For a long time he lay in bed, eyes closed, mind half-fogged still with slumber. He realized that he had forgotten to draw the blinds, and that it was daylight streaming in that had awakened him. That brought him up with a start. His window was so situated that no sunlight reached it in the mornings. So it had to be fairly late. And this was his day for seeing the kids —

He sprang out of bed in a hurry, regretting the impetuous leap the moment the first twinge of pain shot through his stiff, musclebound body. He ached all over. Feeling like a man of ninety, he went to the window and drew the blind. Down below, in back, a cluster of tanned people were splashing around in the hotel's swimming pool.

Lyle found his watch on the dresser. Ten minutes after one. He winced. He was supposed to be at Donna's around two. and Pasadena was way to hell and gone up eastward. Every minute he wasted now was another minute peeled from the precious few Donna would let him have with the kids.

He went into fast action. A quick shower, a shave — his face was sore in a couple of places from the fight — and some fresh clothes. There were little nicks and scratches and bruises all over him, souvenirs of his two tumbles in the hay with Lorayne the night before.

Breakfast would have to wait till some other time. He tied his shoelaces, swallowed a couple of aspirins, and left. The sun was blazing furiously outside. He vaulted into the car and got it moving.

Living in Pasadena had been Donna's idea, not his. Sure, it was pretty, but it was too far from the center of things. He hadn't argued too strongly about it. He was able to do a lot of his work at home, and only had to make the pilgrimage to his Culver City office two or three times a week. And there were advantages to living outside of town, anyway. You missed some of the social events you wanted to get to, but you missed a lot you didn't want to get to. It was very easy to duck a dull party in Pacific Palisades when you explained that you lived umpteen miles away in Pasadena.

Now he cut north till he reached the Hollywood Freeway and buzzed down to the interchange with Arroyo Seco, downtown. Then miles and miles on the freeway, through godawful

Mexican slums and glowing suburbs, till Pasadena drew near. He kept his speed at a steady
sixty and rolled along hypnotically in the left-
hand lane, baking in the sun. For a while he
thought he was going to be sick, but he got himself under control within a mile or two of his
exit. He felt hollow inside, and terribly tired,
and about eight hundred years old.

He left the freeway and drove through quiet
palmy residential streets till he came to the one
that had been his street for six years. The house
still looked spanking new. It was a $70,000 red
brick job with lots of grass and a triple garage,
and he had poured his heart's blood into the
conferences with the architect, and he found it
as easy to think of living somewhere else as he
did to think of parting with an arm or a leg.
Above all else, though, it was the kids' home,
and whoever ultimately got custody of the kids
would get the house too — for a stiff cash settlement.

He didn't enter the driveway, though he
knew there was room in the garage for his little
convertible next to the station wagon he had
bought a couple of years back for Donna. He
parked in the street instead and, feeling foolish
and uncomfortable, went up the walk and rang
his own doorbell.

The familiar chimes sounded. Then the inner
door opened, and he was looking through the
screen door at the familiar features of his wife.

"Hello, Kevin. You're late, aren't you?"

"I came as early as I could. Hello, Donna."

There was no kiss. Lyle stepped inside, a stranger in his own home.

Donna looked good. She was a short woman, five feet three, and Lyle knew what sort of dieting she had to resort to keep from looking dumpy. She didn't look dumpy now. She was wearing a pair of tight white corduroy shorts and a pullover jersey of deep green that complemented her rich auburn hair. With an automatic male reflex he looked at her breasts, and he was a little startled to not see the upjutting mounds of her nipples tight against the thin cloth. So she had no bra on. She had the kind of breasts that didn't suffer from being unconfined, and in her less prim moments she had dispensed with a bra quite often. But the informality was out of keeping now, Lyle thought. The role she was trying to play was mother and custodian, not sleeping partner, *Maybe she's in heat*, he thought, remembering the lawyer's warning.

She noted the direction of his glance, and color came to her face. Lyle tried to keep a poker expression.

"Where are they?" he asked quietly.

"Playing out back. They've got a friend with them."

Nodding, Lyle said, "Okay. You stay away. I'll go play with them."

He walked through the house toward the play area in the back, carefully opening and closing the sliding glass door. He stood on the back patio for a long moment, looking at the three children in the sand box. Two boys, one a neighbor's. A small girl. All three dressed simply in briefs. All three tanned, lean healthy.

They were so busy with their game that they didn't notice the big man who was watching them until several minutes had gone by. And then it was Jimmy, the neighbor's boy, who first made the discovery. Lyle watched him nudge Jeff and whisper to him, as though trying to warn him of the interloper without attracting attention. Jeff shot a quick, worried glance at his father, obviously not knowing what to make of the situation. It was Rhona who broke the impasse, though. Looking around to see what all the whispering was about, she noticed her father on the patio, and exploded from the sandbox with a glad cry of "Daddy!"

The good old Electra complex, Llye thought. He stooped and caught the brown, practically naked little girl as she flashed into his arms. He lifted her high overhead, tossed her up, caught her as she came down. She kissed him.

Jeff was approaching, now, with his friend hanging back in confusion Lyle said, "You go home now, Jimmy. Jeff, come here and give your father a kiss."

He's hesitant, Lyle thought in auguish. *She's been working them up against me. The girl's too young and she loves me too much, but Jeff is getting away from me.*

It was two weeks since the last visit. An eternity for a couple of children whose ages totalled nine years. Jeff came close enough for

Lyle to grab him, though, and at the touch of his father's strong arms the boy's reserve melted away, at least temporarily. For a long minute Lyle held both children tight against him, saying nothing. They looked good. Bigger than he remembered them. He put them down, stepped back, tried to visualize Jeff growing tall and muscular, exchanging his curls for a crewcut, learning baseball and trigonometry and German and the art of sex. And Rhona, already a seductress at four, filling out, sprouting breasts and hips, leaving a trail of broken hearts behind her before she was sixteen. His children. And Donna's.

Hand in hand, the three of them went down to the swings he had built for them. He played with them for a while, pushed them as hard as he dared, then let the swings slow down. Suddenly Rhona turned and asked, "Daddy, are you coming back to live here again?"

"Not — not just yet, sweetie."

"Why don't you come back, Daddy? Didn't you like it here with us?"

"He left because he doesn't like Mommy," Jeff said in what he thought was a *sotto voce*, with a small boy's condescension toward an even smaller sister. "He isn't coming back because Mommy doesn't want him to."

"That isn't so!" Rhona said hotly defending him. She looked up and said. "You do like Mommy, don't you?"

It was an awkward hour. He managed to get them so busy with a game that they stopped asking questions about the changed state of domestic affairs. But he knew it was never far from their minds. They understood what was going on more than he could imagine. They knew a battle was going on behind the scenes.

A battle which I'm probably going to lose, he thought bleakly. Donna had possession of the kids. She didn't deserve them, but rather than risk something messy he had simply chosen to move out, letting her keep the kids until he could legally get them away from her. The trouble was that it could take six months or a year, and a year was a measurable percentage of Jeff's and Rhona's life to date, and in that time Donna could do more damage than he could ever undo. They would always be suspicious of him, always remote.

But at least for now he seemed to be winning them over. At one point Jeff said, "I like playing with you, Daddy. It isn't like playing with Mommy. Mommy's a girl, and she doesn't play rough enough."

"Don't you ever have anybody but Mommy to play with? Any grownup? Doesn't Uncle Bruce come around to play with you?"

"No, Daddy. Uncle Bruce hasn't been here for a long time," Jeff said, and it sounded like the truth.

Lyle was secretly pleased. Uncle Bruce was Bruce Caldwell, a glib-talking press agent who was Donna's lover. Lyle had every reason to believe she would marry Caldwell as soon as she legally could, and if he was keeping away from the house it meant that Donna was belatedly watching her P's and Q's in the hopes of winning the court's sympathy. Of course, he might be visiting her in dead of night. But at least the kids weren't exposed to his greasiness, and that was something of a relief. He didn't want Donna to start building Caldwell up to them as a "new Daddy." Not yet. Not while he still had a chance of getting them.

He played with them until the afternoon grew late and the sun began to drop. Then he took them inside and deposited them in their playroom, and went upstairs to talk to Donna. She had remained in her room all during his visit. At his knock, she padded to the door. She was still without a bra, he noticed.

"All through with them?" she asked.

"For now. I want to thank you for letting us alone during the visit, Donna."

"You don't need to thank me, Kevin. I'm not a complete ogre, whatever you think. They're still your children, and I can't and won't stop you from seeing them."

"I'm glad to hear that. Matter of fact, I'm thinking of coming over here more often. Every other week isn't nearly enough. Suppose I come Wednesday mornings and Saturday afternoons from now on."

"Twice a week? But —"

"They're still my children, remember? And this is still my house, too. I moved out voluntarily, but any time I feel like it I can move back in. And I might just do that, if I think you're trying to set the children against me. I still expect to get custody of them, Donna."

"You do, eh?" She smiled coldly. "Ben's a smart lawyer, but he won't be able to take them away from me. Get used to that fact. You'll have whatever visiting privileges the court will allow, but I'm going to bring them up. So don't threaten to move back in. That'll just make life hell for both of us. We're sensible people, Kevin. We can split up without all the fireworks. It's only right that I be allowed to keep the children."

"So you can let them be run over?"

"Don't be horrible. You seem to think I *murdered* the baby."

"If you hadn't been in bed with Caldwell that day, you'd have seen where he was going."

Her eyes flashed. "I'm under my lawyer's instructions not to discuss that subject with you, Kevin. So let's just drop it right now. If you think you're going to trap me into making any damaging admissions, you're crazy." Abruptly her tone of voice, her expression, her entire bearing changed, becoming more warm, more friendly. "Let's not turn this into a knock-down drag-out battle, Kevin. Let's just make it a relaxed visit between a couple of people who have known each other for a long time. Sit down and let me get you a drink, and let's try to be adult about this thing."

Oh-oh, Lyle thought. *Here it comes. The bitch is in heat after all.* He forced himself to don a polite smile. "Okay, Donna. But just for a while."

He sat. She disappeared into the next room, returning in a suspiciously short time with a tray of daiquiries that she must have fixed up in advance.

He accepted the drink from her. It was cold and good. She knew how he liked them. She knew so much about pleasing him, he thought.

She said, "How are you getting along, Kevin?"

"Managing "

"Are you — lonely?"

"I miss the kids," he said.

"Not me?"

"I miss the old you. The girl I married. I can't say I miss the Donna of the last year or so."

"You think I've changed, then?"

"I know you have. Turning hard. Selfish. Vindictive, even." He smiled into his drink. "A different person with the same body The same lovely body."

"You always liked me for my body, didn't you?" she said. "A pity you never felt really love for me. That was one of the reasons I became so unhappy in recent years. You needed me in bed, but that was all."

"I seem to remember you enjoyed sex too, Donna. It wasn't a one-way proposition."

"Sure I did. But I wanted so much more, and I never got it. Real love. You didn't give it to me, Kevin." She shrugged. "I wake up in the middle of the night and reach for you, all the same. And you aren't there. Does that ever happen to you?"

"I don't like sleeping alone," he said evasively.

"Neither do I. That's why I was thinking as I looked out the window and saw you with the kids —" She hesitated, caught her breath. "Maybe it isn't too late to put things back together, Kevin. Not so much for us as for *them*. We owe them a decent home. And maybe — maybe we could learn to be good to each other too —"

Lyle nearly took her for being sincere, nearly let himself go into an emotional cadenza of reconciliation. But then he remembered the look on her face the day he had found her in bed with Bruce Caldwell, remembered the fishwife obscenities she had shrilled at him, remembered all she had said and done in the succeeding days until, unable to stand watching her metamorphosis into something hateful, he had moved out. She didn't mean a word of what she was saying now. She had hot pants, that was all, and she wanted to use him as an animated candle to soothe her lusts, and then to employ the whole incident as a weapon against him in the custody proceedings. Drunken, lust-crazed, smashing into her bedroom to claim his lapsed marital rights — he could just see her building the story now. Her word against his, and the court sympathetic to a mother.

She was very close to him, now.

"Kiss me," she whispered. "The way you used to, Kevin." And she sidled up to him on the couch, taking one of his hands and placing it on her chest so he could feel the ripe flesh an eighth of an inch away, taking the other hand and locking it between her thighs. She glued her lips to his and wormed her way onto his lap, try- ing to open his clothes with one hand and get her shorts off witth the other. He waited until she had wriggled out of the shorts and, breath- ing hard, was straddling him.

"No," he said, and stood up.

She went tumbling off his lap and landed, her buttocks *splatting* against the carpet, her legs going in different directions. She sat there, hatred blazing in her eyes: naked below the waist, with the ripeness of her belly bare to him, the curling auburn hair, the soft thighs he had stroked so many hundreds of times.

"You — you —" she spluttered.

"What would the court say, Donna? Hearing that you had tried to have sexual relations with your estranged husband? They won't like that."

"I was trying to patch things up — but now, you can rot in hell before —!"

"Sure, sure," he said. He felt quite calm. "Here. I'll help you up, and you can put your pants back on. You ought to get into the habit of wearing underwear, too. The mother of small children should cultivate modesty."

She picked up her shorts and turned her back to put them on. He eyed the lushness of her bare buttocks before they disappeared be- neath tight corduroy. He was doubly glad he had been with Lorayne the night before. Other- wise he would never have been able to resist

Donna's appeal.

She seemed to realize that too. Turning, she smiled crookedly and said, "You can be pretty smug, knowing you have some young tramp as a steady lay. But you'll be whistling out of the other side of your mouth when the court gives me the children!"

"You're inventing things, Donna."

"Am I? I know you too well, Kevin! You can't tell me that you've gone two whole months without sex, and still can throw me off your lap that way! Even if I had poisoned your children, you'd still have laid me just now, because that's the way your body works. You couldn't have said no the way you did unless you were getting it regularly."

"Draw any conclusions you like." He straightened his clothes, headed toward the door. "Thanks for letting me visit," he said with heavy sarcasm. "I'll be back on Wednesday around eleven, unless Naumann wants me at the office. Don't try any tricks. If you pull a vanishing act with the kids, I'll get a court order."

She looked at him stonily. "I won't stop you from seeing them. Once a week."

"I'll be here on Wednesday, and again on Saturday. And pretty soon it'll be you who comes making the appointments to see them." He scowled. "So long, Donna."

He walked out without attempting to say goodbye to the children — he was too angry for that — and drove quickly away. Anger made him careless, but he held the road. Donna's transparent trick was beneath contempt. But now he knew the situation was dangerous. If she suspected that he had a mistress — and after today she couldn't fail to think so — then she would be doing everything possible to get evidence that would demonstrate his moral turpitude and general unfitness for taking custody of the children.

Which meant that he had to be careful in his dealings with Lorayne.

Very careful. A few more nights like the last one — only with detectives snooping around — and chances of getting Jeff and Rhonda would be down to zero. *Damn Donna*, he thought. *Damn the divorce laws! Damn the whole goddam world!*

CHAPTER FIVE

HE HAD A LIGHT MEAL AT HIS hotel. After having gone close on twenty-four hours with nothing more solid under his belt than a daiquiri and a lot of bourbon, he was just beginning to get giddy and headachy, so food was in order. When he was finished, he went upstairs and dialed Lorayne's number.

She took her time about answering. When she did, it was with a seductively drawled "Hello" that set Lyle's pulse pounding.

"This is Kevin. I just got back from my wife's."

"Was it a nice visit, Kevin?"

"More or less. The kids seemed glad to see me." He hesitated. "Things are getting complicated, Lorayne. Donna knows I'm sleeping with somebody."

"So fast? She doesn't waste time!"

"She's only guessing." Lyle said. "She tried to seduce me this afternoon, and when I wouldn't

be made she began putting two and two together. She knows how much will power I'm
likely to have after two months of abstinence. A
hell of a lot less than I showed today."

Lorayne giggled. "I can imagine."

"So we've got to be careful. I want to go on
seeing you, but I can't do anything that would
jeopardize the custody suit. Donna may slap a
detective on me now to find out all the gory details."

"One day and complications already,"
Lorayne sighed. "Maybe we'd better forget the
whole thing."

He went tense and his knuckles whitened
over the receiver. "Do you really mean that?"

"Of course not, stupid! But I don't want to
get in trouble. How are we going to work
things?"

"We just want to avoid being obvious about
it," Lyle said. "Which means no public appear-
ances together. I'd better stay away from your
club. And no handholding in the Brown Derby or
stuff like that. We can be surreptitious and get
away with it. That's all."

"Let's start being surreptitious tonight,
then."

"What do you want to do?"

"Go swimming," she said.

"Swimming? That's not so smart. A lot of
people at the hotel know me. Let me bring a
strange girl down to the pool in the evening and
they'll —"

"Who said anything about a pool?" Lorayne

broke in. "I hate pools. Especially when you've got the biggest swimming pool in the world just a quick drive westward."

"The ocean?"

"You catch on fast, don't you?"

"Look, Lorayne, that's a hell of a drive, and I'm pretty tired out —"

"Sure. An old man of thirty-six needs his rest. At least fourteen hours a day. Okay, Kevin. See you next month, if you think you'll have recuperated by then —"

"Now hold on!"

"Well? It's a hot night. I want to go swimming."

"It's risky. It — oh, hell. I give in. Swimming it is. How soon will you be ready?"

"It's half past seven now," she said. "Drive by my corner at quarter to eight. I'll be waiting."

The moment he hung up. Lyle regretted having said yes. Moonlit swimming at Topanga Beach or Malibu could be great fun, sure. But he was dead tired, this was Sunday night, and tomorrow it was back to the grind. Nor was it the safest thing for a father of two to be doing. He was a good swimmer, but the Pacific could be treacherous at night.

Still, he was committed. He put on a fresh shirt, paused briefly to consider the necessity of taking a pair of swim trunks, decided against it, and left.

He drove the short distance over to Lorayne's place in a few minutes. He was starting to get the feeling that he was spending this entire weekend behind the wheel of the convertible. How many hundreds of miles had he driven already? But that was the way you lived, in Los Angeles. A day wasn't complete until another fifth or a hundred miles had been clocked up on the dial. It was a hell of a crazy city, he thought. But he wasn't sure he liked the New York City style either — twice as many people crammed into half as much space.

Lorayne was waiting at the street corner. He pulled up at the curb and she grinned and said, "Going my way, mister?"

"Could be. I'm on my way to the ocean like a lemming."

"Lemming sounds like fun. Let me come lem with you."

"Ouch," he said. "Get in before I change my mind."

She jumped in. He made a U-turn, trod the gas pedal to go scooting through a light just as it changed, and they were off.

"Did you bring towels?" she asked.

"I forgot."

"I didn't." She waved the bundle. "Two towels. I think ahead."

"Clever girl."

"And did you bring refreshments?"

"What kind of refreshments?"

"The liquid kind. It can get cold out there at night."

He shook his head. "I've got a gallon tin of gas in the trunk. Want to drink that?"

"Only in an emergency. But the liquor stores

are still open. Slow down at the next corner and I'll pick something up for us."

He pulled over to the curb. She unbelted herself and got out. "How about some brandy?" she asked.

"Fine idea." He handed her five dollars. "Get a pint of cognac. And bring me back some change."

"I hear and obey, O Sahib."

He leaned back, watching her trim form move rapidly away. She was wearing green pedalpushers that beautifully molded the fluid lines of her buttocks. She was a delicious sight, tall and athletic-looking, the gleaming pony-tail bouncing around as she walked. A superb creature, he thought. The sort of girl that it was impossible to think of as other than young and full of exuberant vitality.

Moments later, she returned clutching a small paper bag. She handed him two dollars and some change, and pulled the bottle out for his inspection. He nodded and started the car. Within minutes, they were on the freeway and heading for the ocean.

She seemed to have done this often. He was all set to drive out to the beaches he knew, but she guided him up onto the coast highway, and it was nearly nine o'clock before she said, "Okay. Pull the car off and park it here. We'll have to go the rest of the way on foot."

There was a small parking area to the right of the road. He nosed the car into it, pulled up, and switched off the ignition. He was gratified to see that the close-packed trees overhead would protect the car in case it began to rain; he didn't like to put the top up.

There was no one else around. Hand in hand, they went to the edge of the road, waited for a San Francisco-bound bus to roar by, and darted across to the far side. The restraining wall was only two feet high here. Lorayne clambered nimbly over it. Clutching the bottle, Lyle followed her.

It was a rock descent of several hundred feet, or so it seemed; actually, Lyle knew, it was closer to ninety or a hundred feet at this point. Looking down, he saw a narrow strip of beach, no more than a dozen feet wide, stretching off in both directions. Foamy wavelets came rippling in with muffled booms. An almost full moon gleamed overhead, and was reflected in the water far out almost to the horizon.

He was panting and sweating by the time they reached the bottom. To his surprise, he saw that the beach was bigger than it seemed from above. The steep rock wall curved sharply inward, creating a cave-like hollow some thirty feet deep that was completely shielded from eyes above.

It was a warm, sticky night. Lyle crouched on the damp sand, catching his breath. Lorayne grinned at him.

"Winded?"

"A little."

"Poor old Kevin. You haven't been getting enough exercise." She put her hands on his stomach. "Mmm. Nice and tight. No spare tire. You *seem* to be in shape."

"I work too hard to get fat. But I haven't been active at the gym lately."

"I'll get you in shape," she said. "A nice fist-fight one night, rock climbing the next. Tomorrow we'll do some roadwork. Run from one end of Wilshire Boulevard to the other before breakfast."

He groaned. "And Wednesday we can swim to Hawaii and back. Thursday we uproot palm trees and use them for pogosticks. And Friday you plant me in Forest Lawn."

"We can do the Hawaii swim tonight. Come on, slowpoke!"

She began to undress, tossing her clothes casually behind her. She unbuttoned her blouse, unhooked her bra, and took a deep breath, filling her lungs with air that thrust her breasts upward and outward. Lyle looked admiringly at her as he peeled off his clothing. She was out of her pedalpushers, now, and rolling her filmy panties down. Moonlight made her skin glow. She stood with her legs apart, digging her toes into the sand, stretching voluptuously while waiting for him to finish undressing.

He folded his trousers neatly and laid them on the sand. Naked now, he took her hand and they walked to the water's edge. Lyle looked cautiously in both directions.

"You sure nobody ever comes here?" he asked

"Positive. Don't worry about getting arrested. It's safe here."

"I hope so," he said nervously.

She broke free of him and dashed suddenly into the water, racing outward until the waves were swirling around her buttocks, then diving out of sight. Lyle waded in. Despite the warmness of the night. the water struck him with icy impact. He stood in it knee-deep, shivering.

Lorayne bobbed up some forty feet out. Her silvery laughter tinkled back to him. "Jump in sissy!"

He felt absurd, a cold naked figure with clattering teeth. A breaking wave swept up over his loins, and he yelped. Then he dove grimly forward into the water. The first shock of it against him was miserable, but before he had gone five strokes he realized he was adjusting to it. He stuck his head up, caught sight of Lorayne treading water up ahead, and rapidly came even with her.

"Not so bad once you get used to it," she said.

"You can say the same thing about drinking arsenic."

"This is more fun." She wheeled around, rubbing her back up against him. He felt her taut buttocks pressing against him in the water. He put his hands over her breasts, feeling the firm warmth of her even in the cold. Her hands slipped backward, stimulating him. But he failed to respond to her caresses.

"What's the matter?" she asked. "Going impotent in your old age?"

"It's the cold," he said. "Anyway, I'm not guaranteed to function under water. What do you think I am, a goddam ballpoint pen?"

"You haven't lived till you've done it in the Pacific Ocean," she said.

"Have you?"

"Lots of times." She giggled. "I bet you think I'm an inexperienced almost-virgin."

"I have no conjectures about your sex life whatever."

"Take a guess, Dr. Kinsey. How old do you think I was when I first got it?"

"Eight?" he said.

"Close. I was thirteen."

"What?"

"Just like that little movie star. Only it wasn't some greasy pervert in his fifties who laid me. It was the boy next door."

"Lucky little bugger."

"He was fourteen, and scared stiff. I made him do it to me. I read about it, and wanted to know what it was like. Hurt like blazes, too. But the next time it was okay. He learned fast."

Lyle chuckled. "And all this premature experimenting of yours was taking place just around the time I was getting engaged. It must seem like ages ago to you. And just a handful of years to me."

"Of course, there have been a lot more since then."

"Are you bragging?" he asked.

"Just telling. It's part of my philosophy."

"What is?"

"A relaxed attitude toward sex. I never could understand what all the shouting was about.

Look, it's considered all right for girls to let boys kiss them. And when a boy kisses a girl, he sometimes puts his tongue into her mouth, and they both enjoy it. Well, what difference does it make if he puts another part of his body into another part of hers? It's all good fun, isn't it?"

"You ought to lecture at PTA meetings," Lyle said. "If more little girls shared your philosophy, there'd be less frigid wives today, less rapes, less frustrated people. And about eighty million more illegitimate children."

"Can't make an omelet without breaking some eggs," she laughed. "You have to run the risks." She put her hand to him again as they bobbed in the water. Abruptly, he found himself reacting. The moment she sensed that he was aroused, she let go and paddled away from him.

"Hey! Come back!" he shouted.

"Come catch me!"

He took off after her. But she swam like a porpoise. She headed straight out, almost dangerously far from shore, and it was all he could do to stay the same distance behind her. Catching her was out of the question. He doubled and redoubled his efforts, until he was gasping for breath, but he stayed maddeningly the same gap ahead.

He started to get worried. This was too risky: they both might get too far out. He was just about to call to her, to admit he was beaten and to tell her he was heading in for shore, when she abruptly about-faced and began to swim straight at him without a change of speed.

Don Elliott

He pulled up short, and she came barrelling into him, laughing and panting. He felt her warm, smooth body, felt her put her arms around his waist to try to drag him under. He fought her back. But his more powerful muscles were helpless against her agility. She got his head under water and held it there, locking her thighs around his chest. He tried to break free and got his head above the water long enough to drag in some air; then she forced him down again.

The girl played rough. He battled his way up to the surface and pulled her free of him, but now he was winded and weak, and she seemed still full of life and mischief. He started to swim toward shore. She cut in front of him and pulled him under again. Suddenly he began to cough and splutter; his gorge rose, and he thought he was going to be violently sick.

"Kevin?" she said. "You all right? Hey—"

He shook his head and wheezed for breath. She was up against him in a moment, the tips of her breasts grazing his back, as she held him up. He felt his heart return slowly to its normal pace.

"You okay now?" she asked, worried.

"Just about. Jesus, you show no mercy."

"I was just fooling around!"

"I bet you were." He bobbed away from her. "I'm a family man, Lorayne. Don't murder me. For my children's sake."

She swam toward him. He took her in his arms, and they drifted in until he felt sand beneath his feet. They tossed on the waves for a while. She clung tight to him, her body flush against him. He was stiff with desire, now.

"Let's—go ashore." he panted. "Rest for a little while. Dig into that cognac."

"If you want to."

Hand in hand, they stumbled out of the surf. Lyle wanted to drop down at the edge of the beach and rest, but Lorayne tugged him on until they had reached the shelter of the cave. He flopped down on the sand.

She tossed him a towel. "Here. Dry yourself or you'll get pneumonia."

"Thanks." He towelled himself dry. She stood over him, drying herself. He tossed the towel aside, twisted open the cognac bottle, and took a long pull. She took the bottle from him.

"Good," she said, exhaling.

"Great. But I'm still cold."

"Chase me. It'll warm you up."

She tugged him to his feet and then she was off like a frightened gazelle. Cursing, Kyle ran after her. She moved on land with the same speed as in the water. He followed her for three hundred steps, then paused for breath. She stopped too. He waited a moment, then took out after her again. She darted deftly around him and headed back toward the cave. He followed grimly.

Approaching the cave, she ran into a piece of driftwood and tripped, landing in a tumbled heap. Lyle watched her go down, lovely flesh going every which way. He caught up with her before she could rise.

"Hurt yourself?" he asked.

"Just startled."

"Good. *I'll* hurt you, then." He caught her and dragged her across his knee. She had run him ragged, both in the water and on the beach, and he was half amused, half angry with her. He wanted to show her who was boss.

He bent her over so the pink, tender curves of her buttocks were exposed. Then he brought the flat of his hand down on the bare skin. She kicked and wriggled, but he held her tight. The impact of hand on cheek was delicious. He whacked her again and again, until her buttocks flamed an angry red. He felt himself being carried away by the unexpected pleasure of spanking her. Again and again his hand descended, while a blurred haze of delight filmed his eyes, until finally he realized he might be carrying it too far. He let go of her. She tumbled to the sand, landing on her back with her legs spread.

She had the look of a woman desperate for loving.

Her eyes were wide, her nostrils parted, and her nipples were standing up stiff and tall. Her breasts rose and fell rapidly. She reached out, pulled him down on top of her.

"I love it when you do that," she whispered. Her teeth grasped his earlobe; her hands dug deep into the muscles of his back. She thrust upward, and he met her. A ripple of ecstasy went through her immediately.

"Squeeze my breasts, darling. Hurt me! Hurt

me!"

He took the ripe globes in his hands, as he had done before. Her tongue was in his mouth, now. He plunged deep into the moist core of her. Her heart pounded, from the exertions of the two chases and from the workout on his knee. Sweat and droplets of salt water beaded them both. Sand stuck to their skins.

She sank her teeth deep into his shoulder. Their locked bodies rolled over, so that they lay on their sides, and her buttocks were exposed again. With the hand that was free, he began to spank her again. With each loud clap of palm on skin, she gave another gasp of pleasure. Spasm after spasm of delight shook her. He kept on hitting her. She twisted and thrust one breast to his mouth. Automatically he began to kiss it, caressing the nipple, and as he increased the pressure of his lips against the firm globe of flesh she whispered, "Yes, yes, that's it — harder, darling — until it hurts — I love it when you hurt me, Kevin darling —"

He couldn't hold back any longer. With a muffled moan he plunged against her and ecstasy pounded through him. At the same moment she moved in an absolute frenzy, arching her back and writhing like one possessed. He felt the inner softness of her contracting and clasping him, and then she quivered and went limp on the sand and he reached the peak that instant and it ended.

Cold and wet and covered with sand and totally drained of energy, he sprawled out next to her, body still locked to body. One sentence she had spoken stood out with burning clarity in his mind.

I love it when you hurt me, Kevin darling.

The spanking had made her wild with passion.

She was a very odd girl, he thought. Very odd indeed. The first time, she had kissed the blood from his lips. The second time, she had revelled in the feel of dry twigs scratching her bare buttocks. The third time, she had taken pleasure out of a brutal spanking.

Pain and sex seemed all mixed up in this girl's mind. She was savage. She enjoyed inflicting hurt during the act of love, and she enjoyed being hurt. For her sex wasn't simply a stately gavotte with prescribed rules, as it was for a lot of women. It was a knock-down, drag-out orgiastic revel, with no holds barred. Making love to Lorayne Winant was like making love to a jungle cat.

He thought of Leo Naumann and *his* peculiarities. The collection of whips, the odd rubber garments. Leo was an odd one. His sex life was something straight out of Kraft-Ebing. That wasn't any secret.

Lorayne was just the girl Leo would go for. Lyle had decided that the night before, and now he was positive of it. Part of him was pleased with the chance to dispose of Lorayne. She was altogether too much for him to handle, he was rapidly finding out.

But part of him shrieked out in wild protest

against turning her over to Naumann. *I want her*, that part cried. *I want her all for myself!*

CHAPTER SIX

FTER A LONG WHILE THEY ROSE and dusted themselves free of sand and got dressed. It was late, now, and a cold wind was blowing in from the Pacific. They sat crosslegged in their rock shelter and passed the cognac back and forth until it was all gone, and then, fortified by the alcohol, they began the long climb upward to the level of the road.

He drove with exaggerated care on the hairpin turns of the homeward route. Driving back, their lane was on the outside, and in some places there was no barrier. A missed turn would mean a fatal drop. He stared with grim determination at the road ahead of him, for once grateful that the bucket seats and the safety belts kept the girl from getting too close to him. She was just drunk enough not to care whether they went over the edge or not; he was just sober enough to worry about it seriously.

They made it back to town without mishaps.

Lyle dropped her off at her place just after midnight and was snug in his own bed less than half an hour later.

He was tired beyond the point of sleepiness. He figured he had swallowed at least a gallon of salt water tonight. And Lorayne was enough to tire any man. It had been a hectic weekend, he thought. And a confusing one. He was getting deeply involved with this strange, violent girl, and he didn't like the way the situation was building up. He tried to picture Lorayne as a stepmother for Jeff and Rhona, and failed utterly. Lorayne wasn't cut out to be a devoted wife and mother. She was the sort of wild, fiery creature whose role in life involved midnight swims and strenuous orgies. She couldn't be domesticated. He wasn't sure he wanted to try. But a break would have to come, because he couldn't keep seeing Lorayne if he hoped to make a normal home for his children.

The smart thing, he thought, would be to turn Lorayne over to someone who would appreciate her uniqueness, like Leo Naumann, and to live a life of chasity until the divorce decree. After which he could find some sexy but domestic creature to be his wife and a stepmother for the kids.

That would be the smart thing. But getting Lorayne out of his system, he realized, wouldn't be so easy.

After a while he dropped into an uneasy sleep. At half past eight the next morning, the alarm roused him. He was pleasantly surprised to discover that his muscle soreness had left him; evidently the strenuous life Lorayne was making him lead was agreeing with him. He showered and shaved and breakfasted in the hotel coffee shop, and not long after nine he was on his way to his office.

Leo Naumann's headquarters were in a sprawling stucco mansion in Culver City. The bustling Naumann organization was based there; he had other offices strung out all over the world for his use wherever he travelled. Lyle had a large room on the ground floor for his office.

His secretary was busily typing. She was a well-built girl of twenty-three, a starlet who hadn't made the grade. After flunking her screen tests, she had gone into the Naumann organization, and Lyle suspected was one of Naumann's many mistresses. Lyle himself had never been tempted to fool around with her. She had nice breasts, a pretty face, and a better-than-average mind. But not even at his most desperate had he made a pass at her. Naumann frowned on intramural romances, especially when the girl was one he was interested in himself and the man was publicly known to be married and a father. The last man who had worked for Naumann and made time with a staff girl was working for somebody else, now, at half the salary and twice the hours.

"Morning, Ellen."

The girl turned a bright toothpastey smile on him. "Good morning, Mr. Lyle. Did you have a pleasant weekend?"

"Let's call it an *interesting* weekend, Ellen, and drop it right there." He dumped the galley proofs of the African book on his desk. "God damn it, Ellen, how can you look so frisky on a Monday morning?"

"Why, I like my work," the girl said in surprise. "I enjoy being around Mr. Naumann."

I'll bet you do, Lyle thought. As he started going through his mail, he said, "We're buying the African novel."

"Did you really like it?"

"It'll make a swell film," Lyle parried. "Really tremendous. An epic."

"I'm glad. Mr. Naumann's been worrying about the next book. It's been so many months since he bought the last one. Oh." The girl glanced at a memo pad. "Mr. Collins phoned. He's finished polishing up the script of the circus movie and he's delivering it this afternoon."

"About time," Lyle said. The script was going through its fourth rewrite. It made Lyle feel like a slave-driver to insist on the revisions—he had been on the other end of the desk long enough—but he knew exactly what Naumann wanted in a script, and what Naumann wanted took several writers and a lot of drafts to accomplish. Not that any of them were being underpaid. Collins was the third writer to work on the circus script, and he was getting $2200 a week for what was essentially a polishing job. The trouble, of course, was that he would draw his fat salary for six or seven weeks, and then be idle for eight or nine. Lyle preferred the security of his weekly paycheck, smaller though it might be than Collins' current wage.

His desk buzzer sounded. Lyle pushed the switch and heard Leo Naumann say, "Would you step in here a moment, Kevin?"

"On my way, Leo."

Lyle went down the hall and into Naumann's plushly appointed office. You had to step up to get into it; L.N. enjoyed little regal touches like that.

Naumann was standing in the middle of the carpeted floor, naked except for a pair of boxer trunks. He was holding a metal spring exerciser and methodically flexing it across his back. He was a small man, no more than five feet two, deeply tanned and stockily built. He was about fifty-five. His nose was an imperial beak, his eyes deepset and cold, his black hair close-cropped. Put him in a stiff Prussian uniform, Lyle had thought many times, and Naumann could play a villainous Nazi officer with great success. Naumann had claimed to have spent the war years in a Nazi concentration camp, but Lyle had never been able to decide whether he had been there as a prisoner or as a jailer. Naumann left the matter ambiguous, and Lyle never dared to ask.

"I got a wire from New York last night," Naumann began without a word of greeting. "Bryce is taking a jet this morning. Leaves New York at nine local time, which means it's some-where over New Mexico by now. I have a car at the airport waiting to pick him up. Is it a good book, Kevin?"

"It's got everything."

"Okay. I'm relying on your judgment because this is going to be a rush. Leo Naumann is going to make a quickie movie. A six million dollar quickie, but a quickie all the same."

"What's the idea, Leo?"

"Next year at this time twenty different producers will be making films about Africa. I want to get in there first. I hope to sign the contract with Bryce by noon. Before five tonight the first press releases will go out. Tomorrow I'll begin lining up actors. We'll film in Africa, the whole thing on location except the interiors." Naumann's word-flow stopped. He fixed a baleful eye on Lyle and said, "Give me a three-page summary of the important action by four o'clock, Kevin. Prune away everything but the basics. You know how to do it. That's what I'm paying you for. I also want a list of the ten most important characters, with suggested castings. And recommend a couple of boys who can do the script quickly and well. This is going to be a quality job, make no mistake. But I want it to be hitting the theaters inside of seven months."

Lyle whistled. "You're joking, Leo!"

"I don't joke," Naumann said grimly. He flexed the exerciser one last time and hung it in the closet. He was dappled with sweat. His body was lean and hard, and the tanned skin had the color and something of the texture of old leather. "Come over here," Naumann said, going to his desk.

Lyle took a seat and watched as the producer unlocked a drawer. Naumann took out a manila envelope and flung it across the desk at Lyle.

"Take a look at those," Naumann said brusquely. "Let me know what you think of her."

Lyle opened the envelope and drew out a dozen eight-by-ten glossy black and white prints, and half a dozen four-by-five color prints. They were unretouched photos of a girl — taken, Lyle saw, in and around Naumann's house.

She was nude. She was about nineteen or twenty. The resemblance to Lorayne was striking. The pictures were mostly posed, but there were a few candids. They were all masterpieces of nude photography. The girl was shown in startlingly suggestive poses, designed by a master craftsman — Naumann. Her breasts were high and ripe, her body long and lean, her thighs muscular but sensuous, her buttocks full, invitingly curved. But she lacked a certain something that Lorayne had — the fire, the sparkle. This girl was just a naked girl taking a bunch of fancy poses. The same shots of Lorayne would have had to be printed on asbestos paper.

Lyle looked through all of them, then said carefully, "Very nice, Leo. Who is she?"

"A friend of mine. You spoke to her on the phone briefly when you called on Saturday. She's been staying with me the past couple of weeks."

"You take these yourself?"

"Of course, idiot!" Naumann snapped. Then, more calmly, he added, "She thinks I am in love with her. Her name is Audrey Reynolds, and she wants to be a movie star. She will do anything to achieve that goal. Like so many others. *Anything.*" Naumann smiled somberly. He had never attempted to hide his sexual aberrations from Lyle.

Lyle stacked the prints neatly. "You like her, eh, Leo?"

"Very much. Tell me, Kevin: is there a part for her in this book?"

Lyle hesitated, trying to run through eight hundred sixty-seven pages of novelistic bilge in one mental flash. "Why — uh —"

"There must be," Naumann said. "We'll write one in if there isn't. I want her to appear in the film."

"Matter of fact," Lyle said, "there is such a part. An important one. Something of a villianness. A sexy white girl born and brought up in Africa. Daughter of an English settler. Full of fire, going around sleeping with everybody. There's one torrid scene where she's bathing nude in the jungle and tries to seduce a gorilla. Honest to God. It'll never get past the Code."

"The Code can be broken. *Does* she seduce the gorilla?"

"No," Lyle said. "The ape get cold feet. But then along comes the hero, and she seduces him. And then in the end when the natives rise up she gets raped by about three hundred of them, and crawls off into the jungle in a daze and is killed by a lion."

"Wonderful! Wonderful!" Naumann's eyes were gleaming. "This is just the part I wanted for her! She will be fabulous, Kevin. A new star born overnight. I can see that gorilla scene now. The girl's eyes just slits of lust, as she comes naked toward the gorilla a strategic vine hiding her boobs or something like that — a rear view showing as much of that gorgeous backside as we dare — the whole thing for the overseas prints —"

Lyle remained silent during Naumann's rhapsodic vision. When the producer had finished describing the scene, Lyle said quietly, "It sounds great, Leo. Absolutely spectacular. But tell me this: are you one hundred percent committed to using this girl of yours?"

"What?" Naumann looked dumfounded. "Of course I'm going to use her!"

"Even if there's someone better?"

"Who better?"

Lyle wondered whether or not he was making a big mistake. But he had to forge ahead now. "There's a girl I happen to know, Leo, that I was going to introduce you to anyway. She's two-legged dynamite. The part is made for her. No matter how good you tell me this dame is, I'm sure this one is better."

Naumann wasn't accustomed to having his plans upset in this way. He looked stonily at Lyle and said, "Are you trying to interfere with my casting of this picture?"

"I'm trying to help make it as great a picture

as it deserves to be," Lyle said glibly. "Don't make up your mind till you've seen Lorayne."

"Why should I hire a stranger? I —"

"I tell you, Leo, Lorayne is incredible. Just from these photos, I can tell you that she's got it all over this girl of yours. And she's also hungry to make a hit in the movies. She too will do anything. *Anything.*"

Naumann still looked displeased, but less so. "Are you speaking from first-hand experience?"

"Frankly, yes." Lyle reddened. "She's too much for me, though. She's your kind of woman, Leo. And the kind you want for your movie. Do me a favor and take a look at her. If I'm wrong — if I'm wrong you can fire me."

"And if you're right? A raise?"

Lyle scowled. "Leo, I want to see this girl get somewhere in the movies. I'm not out for myself. I just think it's a damned shame to pass up this chance to latch on to a great star of the future. And a spectacular lay besides."

"She must have had a powerful effect on you, Kevin. You don't often talk to me this way."

"I don't often have reason to. Will you take a look at her?"

"All right. But the part still belongs to Audrey until I decide otherwise."

"Naturally, Leo. Naturally. I'll phone her now and see if she's free for tonight. If she is, what arrangements do you want me to make with her?"

"Bring her to my house tonight around nine."

"What about Audrey?"

"Let me worry about her," Naumann snapped. "Go call this paragon of yours, now. And then get busy on that synopsis. I need it by four."

Lyle left the great man's presence and returned to his own office. He realized irritably that he was trembling and sweaty. Well, he was out on a limb for sure, now. He had butted into Naumann's private schemes, contradicted the producer, generally acted pushy and officious. If Lorayne failed to deliver the goods, now, he'd be in bad with Naumann for a long time.

But Lorayne would deliver the goods. The memory of her writhing in delight on the cold sand the night before was enough to assure him of that.

He picked up his phone and dialed Lorayne's number. The phone rang half a dozen times before a sleepy voice said, "H'lo?"

"This is Kevin, Lorayne."

"Who? Oh. 'Scuse me. I haven't awakened yet, Kevin. What time is it?"

"Ten in the morning. Go splash some cold water in your face and then come back. I've got something important to ask you."

"Keep talking. I'm waking up."

"Okay. How easily can you get out of appearing at the club tonight, baby?"

"Why?"

"Can you get out?"

"I suppose. I just tell them I'm sick, or I sprained my ankle over the weekend, or something. But they'll dock my pay, and they'll be sore. What's the scoop?"

"Well, if you could get yourself free tonight, you might find yourself in a more lucrative line of work."

"Meaning what?"

"Meaning how would you like to play the second lead in Leo Naumann's next big picture?"

"Huh?"

"The part is made for you, baby. There's this jungle wildcat of a female living in Africa. Seducing people right and left. A juicy nude bathing scene. And a gimmick with you trying to lay a gorilla. Probably some swinging on vines, too. It calls for a sexy, fiery blonde with no inhibitions at all. It fits you to a T."

"Lyle, you're joking —"

"It's your big break. It'll pay you fifty or sixty grand, not to mention a free trip to Africa. And from here on you'll be in hot demand. They can make a million pictures around you. A passionate Indian squaw getting revenge for the murder of her brave. A determined spy running the Reds a merry chase. A sexy tramp setting a quiet university on its ear. Now that I'm started, I could think up fifty plots for you once you're established. There's only one catch."

"What?"

"Naumann's already got a girl for the part. His current mistress, a girl named Audrey something. I saw a bunch of nude photos he took of her. She's a blonde with a nifty pair of boobs. Looks a lot like you, matter of fact, but her face isn't as nice. And she doesn't give off that crackling sexiness that you have. She's just a star-struck kid who's willing to let Naumann lay her eight different ways from Sunday so long as he makes her a star."

"But if the part's assigned —"

"I told him you could do it twice as well. He got a little sore, but he's curious. He wants me to bring you over to his place tonight for some auditioning."

"In front of the camera or in the bedroom?"

"Probably the bedroom," Lyle said. "I'm warning you to be prepared for anything. But if you perform for him the way you did for me last night, you can figure on getting a contract to-morrow. Just show Naumann a good time in your own inimitable way. Poor old Audrey what's-her-name will be outside looking in."

"Do you really think I have a chance, Lyle?"

"You'll wow him. Will you tell the club you're sick?"

"Sure thing."

"Okay, then. I'll pick you up around half past eight and drive you over to Naumann's."

"What should I wear?"

"Dress informally. The silk blouse and torea-dor pants combination's good enough. It's what's underneath that interests Naumann."

"I don't know how to thank you for this, Lyle. If it all works out well, I'll always be grateful to you. I'll never forget this."

"Save the gratitude for after the contract's signed, sweet. I've got to get some work done around here now. See you tonight."

"So long, Kevin."

He stared at the telephone for a moment after he had hung up. A twinge of something like regret passed through him. The step was taken, now. Naumann was certain to be fascinated by Lorayne, and that was the end of her so far as Kevin Lyle was concerned. *It was grand*, he thought. *A two-night affair. Well, I'll still have the memories. And Leo will be indebted to me for introducing her to him. She was too rich for my blood anyway. Too hot to handle. Leo's kind of woman.*

He sighed.

Then he rolled a sheet of paper into his typewriter and began to type out the synopsis.

CHAPTER SEVEN

LEO NAUMANN'S RESIDENCE was a Beverly Hills mansion in the grand tradition. It was a big, starkly modernistic palace set in the middle of enough land to build a luxury hotel on. The broad lawns surrounding it were as meticulous as a putting green. A row of nine-foot evergreens, trimmed within an inch of each other, served as a living wall for the property, totally shielding it from prying eyes. Two magnificent palms rose in front of the house like sentinels.

The house was a gorgeous display piece. It had cost Naumann a six-figure sum to erect, back in 1950 when he hadn't really had that sort of money to spend. The Leo Naumann of 1950 had nothing much besides his pre-war European reputation, his two undistributed post-war films, and a fistful of interesting properties. But building the house had served notice on the world that Leo Naumann was ready to make it take cognizance of him. By the end of that year, his two undistributed films were out of the can and into five hundred theaters; by the end of the next, he was collecting academy awards galore for *Those Were The Years*, and he owned the house outright.

Lorayne gasped in awe as Lyle pulled into the driveway. "I've never *seen* a house like this!"

"Be sure to tell that to Leo. He can live for days on the compliments people pay his house."

Naumann's chauffeur, an elegant Castalian named Perez, stalked out from the garage and flashed a professional smile. "Good evening, Mr. Lyle. If you'll allow me to park the car for you —"

"Thanks, Perez." Lyle and Lorayne unbelted, leaving the Spaniard to put the car away. They went into the house. An obsequious butler greeted them at the door.

"The mahster is in the study, sir," the butler said unctuously. "You know the way?"

"Of course, Jones."

"Very good, sir."

The butler departed, bowing. Lorayne said, "Is he for real?"

"In a way. He's an English actor who used to play butlers in B movies. Leo offered him more to do some *real* buttling than the movies ever gave him, so he became a butler. He tries to deny he was ever anything else, now."

Naumann's study was a gigantic room, thirty feet square, each of the four walls lined from floor to ceiling with books. Many times, while waiting for Naumann to make his appearance,

Don Elliott

Lyle had studied the books in the shelves. They seemed to be thrown in haphazardly, in no apparent order. And they were in nine or ten different languages. It was reasonable to expect a cultured European like Naumann to have a reading knowledge of French, Italian, and perhaps Spanish, besides his native German and his adopted English. But Portuguese? Polish? Russian? Czech? Hungarian? Lyle half expected to find books in Jananese, Basque, and Gaelic on the shelves too. Naumann's linguistic range was fantastic. As were some of the books. About one out of five in the room was erotic, Lyle estimated.

As Lorayne and Lyle entered, Naumann rose and came toward them. He was dressed in plaid Bermudas and what looked like a satin shirt in fire-engine red. Standing behind him was the girl Lyle had seen in the photos. She looked more interesting in the flesh than in two dimensions, but she still wasn't in the same league as Lorayne when it came to sheer animal magnetism. This girl had the right figure, the right everything, but she lacked the intangible extra that made Lorayne such an irresistible sexpot.

There was a little moment of frozen silence as the four people confronted each other. Lyle looked at Audrey, sizing her up. Naumann stared at Lorayne in open appraisal. Lorayne, after a quick glance at Naumann, turned her attention to Audrey, as though measuring the caliber of her competition. And Audrey returned Lorayne's gaze coldly, almost defiantly. It was going to be an awkward evening, Lyle thought uncomfortably. Why did Naumann have to have Audrey around at a time like this?

"Good evening, Kevin," Naumann said amiably. "And this is your most charming friend, Miss — Miss —"

"Winant," Lyle supplied. "Lorayne Winant."

"Lorayne Winant. Yes." Naumann nodded slowly. "And this is Audrey Reynolds. Audrey meet Kevin Lyle, my story editor and general right-hand man. And his friend Miss Winant."

"How do you do," Audrey said with coldly mathematical precision of enuciation.

"Pleased," Lyle said hollowly.

There was a moment of sticky silence. Lyle was perfectly willing to let it endure forever; this was Naumann's party, and Naumann would have to bear the responsibility for keeping it going. After the brief pause, the producer said, "What will you two be drinking. Kevin, you probably want daiquiris, am I right? And Miss Winant?"

"A daiquiri will be fine for me, too," Lorayne said.

Naumann tinkled a little bell on his desk. The butler entered gravely.

"Daiquiris for four, Jones," Naumann said.

"Very good, sir."

The drinks arrived with astonishing speed. As they took their first sips, Naumann said, "Would you like to see the rest of the house, Lorayne?"

"I'd love to. It's the most beautiful house I've

ever been in. And I'm not saying that just to
compliment you, either. It's the truth."

"The house is my hobby," Naumann said.
"Come."

Quite casually, with old world gallantry, he
extended his arm to Lorayne. They started out
of the room together, Lorayne several inches
taller than the movie magnate. Lyle turned to
Audrey.

"I suppose we're invited too," he said.

"I suppose." Aurdey sounded bitter, and with
good reason. She didn't seem tremendously in-
telligent, but she was smart enough to spot the
gleam in Naumann's eye and realize that she
was an the verge of getting dumped.

He and Audrey followed the other two out.
The house was old hat to both of them, and so
they merely trailed along through the art gal-
lery, the floodlit swimming pool patio, the hall of
Roman statuary, the music room with its ninety
speakers, and all the rest of the regal dwelling
Naumann had put together. The one room they
did not go into — Naumann bypassed the closed
door without a word — was the Amatorium,
where the movie producer amused himself sexually. Lyle had only seen it twice, both times
when Naumann had had too much to drink and
was in a boastful mood. It contained — besides a
triple-width bed — an astonishing collection of
phallic statuettes and erotic paintings, and an
enormous closet full of odd implements used in
perverse sex practices. Not to mention a collection of whips that ranged from a feather-thin

tickler to a cat-of-nine-tails that could be used to administer a fatal flogging.

As they stood in a corridor pretending to admire Naumann's collection of Japanese scrolls, Audrey said, "Have you been with Leo long, Mr. Lyle?"

"Seven years on the payroll. Before that I did some script work for him when I was free-lancing."

"He thinks the world of you, you know. He's always talking about you. Kevin says this, and Kevin thinks that. The other day he said you were indispensable to him."

Lyle smiled. "Really, now? I sometimes get the feeling that I'm very dispensible. Times when I figure I can go back to free-lancing the next day, for all Leo cared."

"Don't let him fool you. He just tries to keep people off balance that way. He's the same way about handing out parts in his movies."

"Oh?" Lyle said cautiously.

Audrey nodded. "For instance, you know, I'm supposed to get a big part in Leo's next picture. Not the circus picture, the one after that. I think it's going to be about Africa. He definitely promised me a starring role. My first. But ever since he first brought the subject up, he's been ducking giving me a contract. Telling me to wait. But promising me I'll have the role. I wish he'd be more definite — in writing."

Lyle felt uncomfortable. "Well, that's the way he is, I guess. Likes to keep people guessing."

"Your friend Miss Winant is very pretty,"

Audrey said, changing the subject abruptly and yet perhaps not really changing it at all. "Is she an actress?"

"Lorayne? Oh, no, she dances in a nightclub."

"But she wants to be in the movies."

"I suppose," Lyle said evasively. "Every pretty girl wants to be in the movies. But I think she's happy to stay at the night club. Less uncertainty that way."

"Leo was impressed by her," Audrey said. "I think you may have some trouble on your hands. He's got that gleam in his eye."

Lyle forced a smile. "What intentions Leo harbors toward her don't bother me. I don't own the girl. She's just a friend of mine."

"Yes, that's right. You're married, aren't you?"

"For the time being."

"And Miss Winant's just a casual companion. So you don't have to worry if Leo goes after her. It isn't as though he wanted to sleep with your wife."

"You sound awfully calm about Leo," Lyle said. "Doesn't it bother you that he should take an interest in other women?"

Audrey shrugged lightly. "I understand Leo. I know he was never made to be monogamous. He has other women coming here a couple of times a week. I just look the other way. Because I know that they're just casual amusements for him, and when he's finished with them he'll always come back to me."

Her naive confidence made Lyle want to

laugh. But he held it in. "How long have you been associated with Leo?" he asked.

"I first met him about three months ago. But it's actually only three weeks that I've been liv-ing here with him. Four weeks on Friday. We're going to get married in September, Leo says."

Lyle's eyebrows rose. Naumann did get mar-ried from time to time — he had had three wives in Hollywood, and perhaps as many before he came to America — but the marriages had a way of quietly fizzling out after nine or ten months. It was as though he felt that he needed a wife to bolster his status as master of this mansion, but never could find the right one. Lyle wondered how the entry of Lorayne would affect Audrey's chances of marrying Naumann. *The poor kid*, he thought.

"It won't be easy, being Leo Naumann's wife," he said.

"Oh, I understand the difficulties," Audrey said gaily. "But I intend to be the first Mrs. Naumann who gets to celebrate any anniversa-ries. You see, I know how to handle Leo's — ah — peculiarities. If he wants to have other women, I'll let him. I don't have the right to mo-nopolize him. Of course, I'll have lovers too, on the side. I'll be very sophisticated about it all. Because I know that Leo will continue loving me, that he'll always come back to me when he's tired of those other women. And, of course, there's the movie thing. Once my career is launched, I'll be set for life."

"You have everything figured out neatly,"

Lyle said. He felt choked with pity for this girl who was going to get hurt so badly.

They walked on a little further, and then the tour of the house was complete, and they were back in the study having some refills. Lorayne was enthusing about the house, quite sincerely — though Lyle could tell from her hyped-up, flushed appearance that she was tremendously excited over the now very real prospect of appearing in a Leo Naumann production. She was doing a lot of drinking. So was Audrey. Naumann, a moderate drinker at best, was holding a glass but taking only occasional sips from it. Lyle cautiously remained sober himself.

Conversation went on in a desultory way for a while longer. Naumann was no longer bothering to hide his interest in Lorayne; they were together on a couch, his head pillowed against her breasts as he talked of his grandiose plans for the distant future, the cycle of Dostoievsky films he intended to make beginning around 1970, the film version of *The Decline and Fall of the Roman Empire*, the definitive movie biography of Christ. Lyle and Audrey were left out of the conversation, off at the side.

About half past ten, Naumann rose suddenly. "Kevin, Audrey, would you excuse us a moment?" he asked. "There are some poems I wish to read to Miss Winant — alone."

The inevitable had happened. Lyle and Audrey bowed to it gracefully enough, and Naumann and Lorayne left the room. Lyle walked to the corridor and watched them go down the hall and disappear into Naumann's Amatorium.

Audrey was standing beside him. "So they're going to do it," she said.

"You sound upset. I thought you were going to be sophisticated and adult about Leo's affairs."

"Yes, but — oh, hell, I'm dizzy. Hold on to me a second, will you, Kevin?"

She swayed. He caught her shoulders, and she lurched up against him. He felt the fullness of her breasts flattening into his shirt.

"Take me down the hall — my room — want to lie down. Had too much to drink."

The sounds of giggling laughter came out of the Amartorium. Ignoring them, Lyle helped Audrey out of the study, and in the opposite direction into her bedroom. He let go of her and she flopped down on the bed, her skirt going up above her knees.

"Lock the door," she said in a quite sober voice.

There was a bolt. He rammed it home. He had half expected something like this to happen when Naumann finally went off with Lorayne.

"Turnabout is fair play," Audrey said. "Leo will be busy with her for the next two hours. Help me off with my clothes, will you?"

Lyle moistened his lips uneasily. He didn't want to break his rule about getting involved with Naumann's women. Even the cast-offs. But — hell, this was Naumann's fault, leaving them alone together. He could visualize the explanation he would give. "I couldn't help it, Leo. I had to keep her amused somehow while you were with Lorayne."

He advanced toward the bed.

Audrey had her panties off already. They were dangling around one ankle, and she kicked them to the floor. Then she rolled over on her stomach and ordered him to unzip her dress. He helped her out of it. Bra, stockings, garter-belt followed in short order. Naked, she looked up at him, her tawny body already rippling with desire. He remembered the photos of her he had seen. Yes, the same creamy breasts, the stiff nipples in their big aureoles. But now she was in motion, churning her thighs and buttocks. And there was the sweat-smell, the lust-smell, the woman-smell.

He stripped in a hurry. She drew him down on top of her, her legs opening, her smooth thighs slipping around his body. He made no immediate attempt to take her, just caressing her for a moment, until she impatiently seized him and guided him to the seat of warmth. A low throaty sound of pleasure escaped her lips as they began to move.

She was good. She had been trained by a master of the art, after all. She knew which muscles to contract, she knew what sounds to make, she knew what positions to assume, she knew what to do when.

But there was something missing. After two nights with Lorayne, this girl couldn't match up. Audrey knew all the theory, and she had all the bodily equipment to put it into practice. But she lacked that intangible something. Audrey was just a girl going through a well-drilled routine. She was a highly skilled sexual athlete, that was all.

But Lorayne —

Lorayne was different. Making love to Lorayne, Lyle thought, was like making love to Woman Incarnate. To Eve herself. When you joined your body to Lorayne's, it was like plugging into a live socket. Lorayne radiated erotic electricity; she tingled; she throbbed. Audrey was an interesting piece. Lorayne was an unforgettable experience.

Feeling oddly remote and detached, Lyle glanced down at the naked girl gasping and panting beneath him. Her eyes were closed, her mouth hung slack and moist. She was holding him tight, now, and then she began to shiver and shake. Suddenly her breath left her and she quivered violently and reached her culmination, and Lyle, the detached, aloof observer, allowed himself his little moment of excitement then and joined her in the pleasure plunge.

A few minutes later, as soon as she had calmed down, he slipped from her grasp and padded into the bathroom that adjoined the bedroom. When he came out, Audrey was sitting up, a glazed, pleased look in her eyes.

"It's a relief to do it the ordinary way for once," she said, smiling. "I guess I don't need to tell you about Leo and his strange ways."

"I've heard," he said.

"I've more than heard. I've experienced. He's a very sick man, I think. Tying himself up in a woman's corset before he does it. And sometimes he beats me with a little whip. Or makes me walk around on my hands, naked. He's got all the perversions in the book."

"And yet you want to marry him?"

"Oh, I don't really mind the things he does. They're sort of interesting. It's just that I like the good old ordinary way, too. Well, I suppose I'll get plenty of opportunities for that, while Leo's with his women." She rose and cupped her hands over her full breasts and yawned. "We'd better get dressed, now. I wouldn't want Leo to suspect."

Fifteen minutes later, they were back in the study. It was past midnight, now. They sat in opposite chairs, saying very little.

Twenty minutes passed, and then Naumann and Lorayne returned, both of them fully dressed. The only outward sign that anything had gone on between them was Lorayne's expression; Lyle knew her well enough by now to be able to detect the slightly haggard look she adopted when she had been well and thoroughly loved, and she looked that way now.

"I hope you two weren't too bored waiting for us," Naumann said. "I was showing Miss Winant some of my treasures."

"We amused ourselves," Audrey said.

Naumann nodded absent-mindedly and looked at his watch. "Well, it is quite late. Kevin, there will be much work for you tomorrow, now that the contract is signed. We're going to get scripting and casting under way just as soon as we possibly can. And I want to thank you for bringing your charming friend to visit us tonight. I do hope we'll see much more of you, Miss Winant."

Naumann and Audrey showed them personally to the door. The chauffeur had already brought Lyle's car out and left it in the driveway. They buckled themselves silently into their seats.

"Well?" Lyle asked finally.

"I can't ever thank you enough," she said.

"You're in, huh?"

"Like Flynn." She grinned. "Leo Naumann is the most fascinating man I've ever met in my life."

"I figured he'd appeal to you. And vice versa. What went on in there?"

"Everything. Oh, Kevin, I couldn't begin to describe it. He's—well, perverted. But not disgustingly so."

"I thought you left Joe Hammond's agency because Hammond was peculiar sexually."

Lorayne shook her head. "Hammond was just a filthy pig. Leo's an artist. He knows exactly how to stimulate a woman. I thought I'd die of excitement in there. Not that I'm criticizing you, darling. I enjoyed every second of the times when we were together this weekend. But Leo's — well — extraordinary."

"The Beethoven of sex, eh?"

"I've never experienced anything like it."

Don Elliott

Lyle nodded. They were a well-matched couple, Naumann and Lorayne. Fit for each other.
He was glad he had brought them together. But
he felt the pang of loss, all the same.

And then Lorayne upset the applecart. "You
want to know something crazy?" she asked.

"What?"

"Even after Leo — even after all I experienced tonight — I still want you, Kevin."

CHAPTER EIGHT

HE WAS SO ASTONISHED HE nearly let go of the wheel.

"You want me?"

Her voice came to him through a million miles of fog. "I know it's crazy, Kevin. I mean, we're practically strangers—it doesn't make any sense at all—but I've known since I got into your car Saturday afternoon that you're the man I've always wanted. Just to *be* with. Not to marry or anything else. Just to keep company with."

He stared straight ahead. "It can't work, Lorayne. There are too many things against it."

"I know. I'll be tied up with Naumann, and you say he doesn't tolerate any competition. And you've got the divorce mess to get done with, and after that the kids to raise. And I'm no good for raising kids. I'd be a lousy wife for you, Kevin. A hell of a swell mistress, but a lousy wife."

"Did — did Naumann say anything to you about the part in the movie?"

"No. Not in so many words. But while — while we were in bed he said that he has big plans for me. First he has to get that poor Audrey out of the picture. Then I guess he'll want me to move in with him."

"And will you?"

"I don't know," she said. "I mean, yes, I want the movie contract, I'll do anything to get that. But once I've got the contract, he can't stop me from moving out, can he? I mean, I wouldn't want to be tied up with him for life. He's like caviar. You can splurge and enjoy some now and then, but you can't live on a steady diet of it."

"You could always pull out on Leo after a while. It wouldn't matter once your career was launched."

"That's what I figured. And then — then I could come back to you, Kevin."

"Even if I'm remarried and trying to bring up the kids?"

"Who would you marry?"

"I don't know. But if I get custody of the kids, I'll be looking for a wife the next day. A good wife. One who loves the kids as much as she loves me, no more, no less."

"Not someone like me."

"I'm afraid not," Lyle said.

"This whole thing is crazy," Lorayne said hollowly. "We ought to get far away from each other before we destroy each other. I belong with somebody like Leo. And you belong with a good motherly type. And here we are scheming and plotting to go on seeing each other. When there actually isn't any room in your future for me, or in mine for you."

He pulled up in front of her house. Nothing had been solved during the ride.

"Do you want to come up?" she asked. "You could spend the night here."

"Thanks, no," he said quietly. "I'm pretty beat. I'd just as soon go on home. And it would look bad if Donna has detectives following me." *Christ woman*, he thought, *haven't you done enough sexing for one night?"*

Disappointment was vivid on her face. He squeezed her hand and they looked at each other for an inarticulate moment, and then she turned and ran inside. He drove slowly toward his hotel, confused and troubled. How had this happened so fast, he wondered? Why did they mean so much to each other after just two days?

Look at it rationally, he told himself, lying sleeplessly in his bed. *She's basically a completely amoral girl. She's willing to sleep with anybody to get to the top. God knows what kind of tricks Joe Hammond tried to pull with her, but other than that she's got no inhibitions at all. So she latched on to me by accident, and got herself introduced to the one man in Hollywood who can really help her, Leo Naumann.*

Okay. She has what she wants now — a lover who can satisfy her most offbeat fancies, and a contract for a big role in a big movie. And me, well, I had a couple of nights of high-

powered sex to brighten my life, and also the satisfaction of having Leo Naumann indebted to me.

Good. So at this point I ought to step out of the picture. Leave Lorayne with her new play-mate, and go back to the business of getting un-tangled from Donna and finding a mother for my kids. Which Lorayne emphatically isn't suited to be.

So why am I getting all emotionally bound up with her? And she with me? We only spell trouble for each other. We ought to play it smart and cool things off right now.

A new idea drifted unbidden into his mind. He found himself concocting a fantasy of giving up the children without a struggle, marrying Lorayne, and starting all over. Naumann would probably fire him. What of it? Once Lorayne was safely launched in her first picture, she would be snapped up by half a dozen eager independ-ent producers. She wouldn't need Naumann any more. Neither would he. He could always go back to writing scripts as a freelancer, and make twenty or thirty thousand a year that way. And Lorayne's income would be fabulous, at least while she was a new sensation.

The gaudy image faded and withered the moment it stood full in his mind. It was the lousiest idea he had had in twenty years, he thought. Turn the kids over to Donna? Let them be brought up by her and that snake Caldwell? Be permitted to visit them ten weekends a year, or something like that?

And he didn't care for the other end of the deal either. Marry Lorayne? Spend the next forty years in bed with that sexual dynamo? She'd burn him out before he was forty. He couldn't handle her. Besides, the future didn't look too bright for Lorayne. What would she be, once her beauty had faded, once her breasts had begun to sag and wrinkle, once her flesh had lost its lushness and grown flabby?

Nothing. That's what she would be.

Nothing.

Lyle rolled over, jammed his face into the pillow, and let sleep blot out the unanswerable questions that assailed him.

He got to the office early the next morning. The place was hectic. The contract for filming of the still untitled African novel had been signed yesterday afternoon, and now the public-relations wheels were starting to turn. Press releases had to be sent out. Spadework done. A title found in a hurry, both for the novel and for the film. Little of this was Lyle's department, but he was caught up in the general frenzy. He spent an hour pounding out a revised version of the synopsis he had done yesterday. The screenplay's structure was beginning to take shape. By the end of the week, writers would be called in to begin the treatment and the expansion.

At half past ten, Leo Naumann sent for him.

Lyle entered the great man's office and waited patiently while Naumann finished a phone conversation. Naumann snapped out an epithet and slammed the phone down.

"That was New York," he said. "The publishers. They've just clinched a paperback reprint deal for the book, and they wanted to know when the movie was going to be released. I told them next March at the latest and they blew their stacks. The paperback people want to put their edition out the day the movie opens. And the hardcover boys figured they had at least fifteen months to peddle *their* edition first. Now they've only got six or seven." Naumann spat. "To hell with them. Money-grubbing bastards. They're getting half of the author's share of the movie money, and half of the paperback money, and they're worried about what's going to happen to their lousy trade edition yet. What do they want? The book's already made them two hundred thousand just on subsidiary rights, and they haven't printed a single frigging copy. *Publishers!* Sit down, Kevin."

Lyle eased himself into a chair and waited patiently while the producer blew off some more steam.

Then Naumann said, switching subjects deftly, "This Lorayne of yours. Can she act?"

"I suppose so. She can learn, anyway."

"Doesn't matter," Naumann muttered. "All she has to do is play herself, and she'll come across. I'm giving her the role, Kevin. And she goes on the payroll next Monday. Seven hundred fifty a week."

"What happens to Audrey?"

"She gets tossed out on her pink little rear," Naumann said, lighting a cigar. "There isn't room in this organization for duplication of talent. Audrey is the same kind of girl Lorayne is, only Lorayne has her beat in every department. Just as you said. So Audrey leaves. I'll find her a contract with one of the big television studios. She won't starve."

Lyle narrowed his eyes and decided to take a big chance. "Don't you think you're getting away a little cheap, hiring Lorayne for $750?"

"She's green talent. I could give her two grand, but then she'd get an exaggerated idea of her own abilities. This way we bring her along slowly. By the time shooting begins, I give her an incentive raise to eight hundred. Then nine hundred. When we bring the picture in, I boost her to a thousand. On her next film, she starts at two thousand. Gradual increments, Kevin, that's the secret. Otherwise by the time she's doing her third film she'll be demanding half a million down and a tenth of the gross." Naumann reached into his desk drawer. "I'm very grateful to you for introducing me to her, Kevin. I want you to have this as a little token of my thanks." He slid a sealed envelope across the table to Lyle, who picked it up and pocketed it without opening it. "You'll find your paycheck's a little heavier on Friday, too. It's a long time since I've given you a raise," Naumann added.

Lyle mumbled a few appropriate words of gratitude and left. Outside the office, he went into the washroom and opened up Naumann's envelope.

It contained a crisp, shiny thousand-dollar bill.

Lyle stared at it in awe. Even in Hollywood, a thousand crackers was a thousand crackers. Even if you were making a thousand a week anyway. It was still dough.

He crumpled the envelope and tossed it into a bowl and flushed it down. A moment later a surge of bitterness flooded through him. He crumpled the bill and extended it toward the toilet bowl. His hand quivered, but he held onto it.

Well done, thou good and faithful pimp! he thought. *You delivered the goods, and now you've been paid. For services rendered. How low can a man sink?*

After a moment of internal struggle, he drew back his hand, smoothed out the thousand-dollar bill, and put it into his wallet. Throwing the bill away would be just an adolescent stunt, he told himself. It wouldn't wipe out the fact that he had served as a procurer for Naumann, a go-between. If he felt guilty about accepting the money, there were plenty of charities who could make better use of it than the toilet bowl would. He walked out, a sour taste in his mouth, and went back to his desk.

He worked right through lunch hour. Things were starting to take shape. He had the structure of the film blocked out, now. The keen story sense that had taken him successfully through twenty movie scripts of his own and a couple of hundred radio-TV shows enabled him to reduce a novel of 500,000 words to manageable and filmable proportions quickly enough.

He had his tentative cast pencilled now. It gave him a little thrill to write Lorayne's name down in the third slot. He had some ideas about the scripting, too. He took them to Naumann later that day, and Naumann shrugged and said, "Okay, call them up and have them stop in here."

He made the appointments. Two writers, at the start. With plenty more held in reserve to polish and repolish the script after the first story conference that ended in a blowup.

By six o'clock in the evening, everything was more or less under control. Lyle tidied up his desk, said goodnight to Naumann — who would be embroiled in phone conversations with New York for at least two more hours — and left.

As he passed through the lobby of his hotel, the desk clerk called to him.

"Message for you, Mr. Lyle."

He took it. The printed form said simply that Miss Winant had phoned at five o'clock, and had left a number at which she could be reached. Lyle's eyes widened as he saw the number. It was one he knew as well as his date of birth.

It was Leo Naumann's home number.

Hurrying upstairs, Lyle dialed it. The butler answered, and Lyle said, "Is Miss Winant there, Jones? Kevin Lyle."

"Certainly, Mr. Lyle. I'll connect you with her in just one moment," came Jones' ineffable bland tones. No hint of surprise on the butler that there had been a change in mistresses overnight. No admission that anything unusual was going on. Lyle wondered what had happened to Audrey.

He heard Jones clicking the receiver until Lorayne picked up her extension.

"Kevin, darling," she said.

"I just got home. Your message was waiting for me."

"Yes. I'm all moved in. Leo phoned me around four in the morning last night and asked me if I would, and I said yes. And he also told me he was giving me a contract for that movie. Seven hundred fifty dollars a week!"

"I heard," Lyle said. He felt a twinge of pain. "So you're all set up, then."

"Isn't it wonderful? I can't ever thank you enough for all this!"

"I wonder what happened to Audrey," Lyle said absently.

"She — she wasn't here when I got here. Not a sign of her or her things. Naumann moves efficiently when he's changing women. Will he get rid of me the same smooth way?"

"You keep on pleasing him and he won't want to get rid of you," Lyle said.

"I hope not. But I still want to go on seeing you, Kevin. Whenever we can."

"You reailze there's an extension phone in every room of that house?"

"You think — oh." She stopped. "It's beginning already, then. The secrecy. The conspiring. Look, Kevin, keep in touch with me. Please?"

"I will," he said. "And congratulations. Give

my best to Leo."

He rung off. *I ought to feel pleased*, he thought. *I've launched her career for her. And now I can try to get my own life back to normal.*

There was a knock on the door.

Frowning, Lyle went to open it. He looked out.

Audrey.

"You son of a bitch," she said. "You stinking bastard."

She looked nightmarish. Her eyes were redrimmed, her hair unkempt, her face sweaty. She smelled of alcohol and rank perspiration. Not at all the well-groomed sex kitten he had gone to bed with the night before.

She came staggering into his room, slamming the door behind her. "Damn manager didn't wanna let me in. I told him I was your sister. He finally gave up."

"What do you want, Audrey?"

"Haven't you heard? Leo tossed me out. Middle of the night, must have been three o'clock. Came into my room and gave me one last piece and told me to pack."

Lyle fidgeted. "I'm sorry to hear that. But don't get the idea it's my fault. I —"

"All your fault," she muttered thickly. "You brought him that whore Winant. All a put-up job. I had a good thing there, and you killed it."

"Look, Audrey —" He didn't know what to say. She was right, one hundred percent right. He had cut her loose from Naumann all by himself, coldly and deliberately, for Lorayne's benefit. Now he had to face his guilt. And the girl. He said, "How did you find out where I live?"

"Looked in Leo's address book. I'm not that dumb."

"And what do you want?"

"You're gonna take care of me. You messed me up, now fix things. With somebody else."

"I work for Naumann. I can't do anything for you. Listen, Audrey, Leo will take care of you. He'll get you a place to live, he'll get you a movie or a television deal —"

"Don't want a thing from him. That dirty bastard. Wouldn't touch his money. Left all my things in storage. I'm moving in here with you. Gonna make you suffer for what you did to me. I'm not so ugly, anyway. You need a woman now that you sold yours to Naumann." Abruptly she pulled open her blouse, unsnapped her bra. Firm full breasts thrust upward at him. She lurched forward. "Here. See, I got a nice pair of knockers too. Take a feel. Come on, grab hold of them." She seized his hands and clapped them down on the warm stiff-nippled globes of her breasts. He pulled back as though she had put his hands on a hot stove.

Laughing drunkenly, she began to peel off her clothes. She had obviously been wandering the streets and crawling the pubs since early that morning; she was sweaty and grimy. Lyle watched dumfounded. In a moment she stood naked before him, her legs spread in a gesture similar to the ones he had seen in Naumann's photos of her.

He grabbed her bare shoulders and shook her roughly. The full spheres of her breasts bobbed and jiggled. "Pull yourself together, girl! Get your clothes on and — no, you'd better sober up first." He dragged her toward the bathroom and turned the cold water on in the shower. He thrust her under the spray. She howled and tried to break loose, but he held her firmly. When he dragged her out, she was shivering and soggy, but clean. He towelled her dry, while she clutched at him and tried to get him to kiss her.

"There," he said finally. "Now get back into your clothes and sit quietly. I'll have some coffee sent up."

"Screw yourself. Bastard. Why'd you have to mess up my life?"

Her red-rimmed, accusing eyes followed him around the room. He had never figured on this, on having Naumann's castoff mistress hanging on his neck like an albatross. He felt on the edge of panic. He had to get this girl out of here, fast. And make sure she never came back.

Still naked, she postured and writhed in a revolting display. The girl had cracked up completely. This was Naumann's fault, not his. Last night Audrey had been talking about marrying Naumann in the fall. And then to be tossed out of the house in the middle of the night — small wonder she had broken up this way. But why come plaguing *him?* Half out of spite, he thought. And half because she had gone to bed with him last night and liked it.

She got up now, rubbing herself against him. He pushed her back into the chair.

"I'll order some coffee."

"Everybody hates me. Naumann. You. Am I so ugly? What is it, anyway?"

"Naumann's a cold-blodded, completely ruthless man," Lyle said. "You aren't the first mistress he's discarded this way. I could have warned you. You just have to accept the fact that —"

But she was too drunk, too hysterical to be reasoned with. She began to cry wildly. Turning away from her, Lyle picked up the phone, asked for Room Service.

"Send up a pot of coffee, will you? Yes, black-coffee, with some cream and sugar on the side. And — just a minute."

He heard the sound of a window being opened. Dropping the phone, he whirled, just in time to see half of Aurdey, just her legs and buttocks, hovering on the ledge of the window. He made a frantic grab for her, got one hand onto the fleshy part of her buttocks, then lost the grip.

She fell.

Five floors.

"My God," Lyle shuddered, as he stared numbly out the open window at the shattered thing on the terrazzo pavement sixty feet below.

CHAPTER NINE

ABRUPTLY HE TURNED AWAY AND ran for the bathroom. By the time he had finished retching fists were pounding on his door. He gulped a glass of water, and then, weak and sweating, made his way to the door. He pulled it open. An army of faces looked in at him: the hotel manager, the desk clerk, bell-hops, elevator boys, guests, chambermaids.

The manager, a dapper man named Mr. Williams, stepped deftly in and closed the door in the faces of the horde of curiosity-seekers. He said, "A woman just fell out of a window on this side of the building, Mr. Lyle. And some of the people at the pool say she fell from your window."

"Is she dead?" Lyle asked in a stupefied voice.

"She *did* fall from here?"

"God, yes, yes, she fell from here! She was a crazy girl and I hardly knew her and she was drunk and jumped out the window while I was trying to order black coffee for her. Ask your room Service operator! He'll tell you I was right in the middle of ordering, and I said 'Just a minute' and turned around when the window opened, and then — oh, God, then she jumped out."

Williams looked grim and thoroughly annoyed that anything so messy as this could happen in his genteel little hotel. "I'll have to ask you to remain in your room until the police arrive, Mr. Lyle."

"Of course. I'm not going anywhere. But is she dead?"

"Killed instantly, Mr. Lyle. The body is quite unpleasant to look at. She fell head first, you know."

"Yes," Lyle said in a hoarse whisper. "I tried to grab her, but I couldn't hang on." He looked down at his right hand in a peculiar way. "I couldn't hang on," he repeated. He shuddered, thinking of that beautiful full-breasted girl lying shattered and bloody on the pavement below. He was remembering the ardor with which she had made love to him the night before, remembering the taste of her mouth, the softness of her thighs, the firm warmth of her buttocks, the woman-smell of her, the tang of her sweat as they thrashed about on the bed together. And now she was dead. Mutilated.

Suddenly he realized he was in very big trouble.

"Excuse me," he said to the manager. "I've

got to call my lawyer."

"Of course, Mr. Lyle."

Lyle picked up the phone with trembling hands. He was beginning to visualize the sort of headlines this thing would make. Naked starlet jumps to death from Naumann executive's hotel room . . . . Naumann's cast-off mistress . . . . the executive separated and awaiting a decree . . . . a statement from the executive's estranged wife . . . . "no comment" from Leo Naumann . . . . yes, the papers would have a field day with it. He'd be famous overnight as the man from whose window Audrey Reynolds took her suicide leap.

He dialed Montereale's office number first, but the lawyer had left. *Please, God, let him be home already. Don't let him be tied up on the freeway in a traffic jam. I need him here, right away.*

On the third ring, Montereale answered.

"Hello?"

"Ben, this is Kevin Lyle. I'm in trouble, and you've got to get over to my place right away."

Montereale said calmly, "Look, Kevin, I'm just sitting down to dinner. Whatever this is, I'm sure it can wait a couple of hours, so —"

"It can not wait," Lyle said. "Get this, Ben: some crazy girlfriend of Leo Naumann's just came busting in here drunk, took off all her clothes, and jumped out my window."

"What?"

"The police are going to be here in five minutes. And you'd better be, too."

"Is this some hashish dream you're having?"

"If it is, newspapers will be having the same dream in the early editions."

"Jesus Christ," Montereale said. "Of all the crazy — okay. I'm on my way over. Try not to say anything to anybody until I arrive."

Lyle hung up. It made him feel better to know that help was on its way. It would take the lawyer ten or fifteen minutes to drive over from his home nearby. The police would cer‑ tainly he here before then. Lyle wondered whether he'd be able to hold them off by himself.

Five minutes later, the room was full of cops — snooping around the window ledge, taking measurements, or just staring malevolently at Lyle. A burly man of about forty introduced himself as Lieutenant Donleavy, and confronted Lyle.

"I'd like to hear your story of just what took place here this evening, Mr. Lyle."

"My lawyer will be here in ten minutes, Lieutenant. I'd prefer to wait for his arrival."

"You can answer a couple of questions, can't you?"

"I'd rather wait," Lyle said, nervously eyeing the notepads that were getting everything down. Cameras were going off, now. They were photographing him, the bed — thank God it didn't look rumpled, he thought — the window, Audrey's scattered clothes.

Lyle fenced with the policemen for a few more minutes. He began to sweat. Reporters would be here soon. What a stinking mess! Why couldn't she have picked somebody else's win‑

dow to jump out of? Don't I have enough throu-
bles as it is, he wondered?

The door opened and Montereale made his
entrance. He was well known to the Los Angeles
police, and they looked at him with a mixture of
respect and sullen dislike. The lawyer looked
cold-faced and angry, now; he hated to be
dragged away from his family at any time, but
he positively detested being yanked out of the
house with the roast beef steaming in the oven.

"Mind if I have a word with my client, Lieutenant?" he said to Donleavy. "Then you can ask
him all the questions you like."

Donleavy shrugged. "Go ahead. But make it
snappy. We've wasted a lot of time already."

Nodding, Montereale said to Lyle, "Come on
into the bathroom."

They went in and closed the door. Montereale turned a look of scathing contempt on
Lyle and said, "You miserable dumb bastard."

"Ben, it wasn't my fault! How could I —"

"Okay, skip it. What have you told these
cops?"

"Nothing. I've been stalling them off with a
lot of hot air."

"All right. Give me the story, and give it to
me straight. Without decorations. I could wring
your neck sometimes, Kevin."

Lyle moistened his lips. "The girl was Leo
Naumann's mistress until last night. Yesterday
evening I went over to Naumann's place and introduced him to a young actress named Lorayne
Winant, a girl I happened to know. Naumann

took an instant fancy to her. This Audrey was supposed to get a big part in Naumann's next picture, but Leo was so taken with Lorayne that in the middle of the night he told Audrey to pack and get out. A typical Naumann operation. This morning I found out that Lorayne is getting a contract for the role Audrey was supposed to do. And that Lorayne is also going to take Audrey's place in Naumann's bedroom."

"Very pretty all around," Montereale commented acidly. "Okay, how did the girl get to come here?"

"She figured I was the author of all her misfortunes," Lyle said. "So she sniffed my address out of Naumann's little black book. Then she went out and got herself stinking drunk, and around quarter after six or so she came knocking on my door. I let her in and she began to spout off about how I had ruined her life, because if I had never introduced Lorayne to Naumann Audrey would still be riding high, etc., etc., etc. Then she started to get amorous. She figured that if Naumann wasn't going to lay her any more, I would have to stand in. Or something. I don't know what was going on in her mind. But all of a sudden she pulled off every stitch of clothing."

"And you laid her," Montereale said.

"Don't be silly. I dragged her into the shower and turned the cold water on her to sober her up. Then I ordered some black coffee for her. They can confirm that downstairs. While I was talking to Room Service, she opened the window and jumped out."

Montereale scowled, his fleshy face furrowing deeply. "That's the whole story?"

"So help me God, Ben." Even as he pronounced the oath, he realized he hadn't told the lawyer that he had gone to bed with Audrey at Naumann's place the night before. But that wasn't really relevant, Lyle told himself desperately. It would only cloud the issue. All that mattered was that a drunken jealous girl had heaved herself out the window in some crazy attempt to get even with the world that had wronged her.

Montereale said, "Okay, then. Let's go out and talk to Donleavy and his boys. Stick to the story you just told me and don't waver at all, and you'll come out of this all right."

"But I can't tell them about Leo and his love affairs."

"Tell them everything," Montereale said sternly. "The first problem we face it getting you uninvolved with this girl's death. After that we can worry about covering things up for Naumann."

They went outside. The policemen were milling around impatiently. Donleavy said, "You got your client all coached now, Montereale?"

"I've listened to his story. I'm convinced that he's an innocent bystander in all this. You can ask him any questions you like."

For the next ten minutes, Lyle was exposed to a battery of rapid-fire questions, while two police stenographers got everything down. He

answered each question straight, without eva·
sion. It was almost a positive pleasure to give
honest answers to questions in Hollywood. *Yes,
the girl was a protege of Leo Naumann's. No, I
didn't know her personally. Last night was the
first time I ever met her. Yes, 1 was responsible
for finding the actress who pushed the dead girl
out of her role. That's part of my job, helping to
cast Leo Naumann's pictures. No, I didn't make
any sexual advances to the girl when she came
here. She took off her own clothes. I didn't touch
them. She was absolutely stewed.*

He stuck unwaveringly to his story. It was so
easy to tell the truth, he thought wearily.

At length Donleavy said, "That's about it.
We're through with you for now, Mr. Lyle."

"You aren't going to take me into custody?"

"No need to," Donleavy said. "It's pretty ob·
vious suicide. If the autopsy shows a big per·
centage of alcohol in her blood, it'll back up the
story you told. And the doc will be checking to
see if she had any sex just before she died, too.
It's going to be bad for you if she did."

"She didn't have any with me," Lyle said.

Montereale said, "Are you through with my
client now?"

"I just told you so," Donleavy replied. "But
there are some reporters outside who —"

"Okay. Give me half a minute." Montereale
turned to Lyle and said, "Does that other room
lock?"

"Why, yes, but —"

"Okay. Go in there and lock yourself up. Stay

in there and don't come out, no matter what, and don't say a word through the door. I'll tell you when to come out. Just lie down and relax."

Nodding numbly, Lyle went into the room he used as his study and clicked the lock shut. He dropped down on the couch, feeling that every nerve in his body was frayed and wearing through.

He closed his eyes. And once again he saw Audrey standing before him, naked, her hands cupping her breasts, thrusting them upward and outward at him. Saw the hard points of her nipples bursting with drunken desire. Saw the sensuous round of her belly, the sleekness of her bare hips. Saw her capering erotically, exposing the secret places of her body to him. Then saw her hanging suspended on the window ledge, her head and breasts already out, her legs dangling in the room. Felt the impact of his hand on her buttocks, the sticky sensation of her firm flesh sliding out of his grasp, her legs kicking out as she launched herself into space, the dreadful sound a moment later as she cracked into the pavement —

He felt sick.

He clung tight to a couch cushion until the spasm passed. To his amazement, he felt his desire beginning to rise. The nervous tension that gripped him was stimulating him erotically. The naked girl, the violent death, had churned up his emotions, and now he wanted to pierce some soft body, to ride out the storm in his soul on a clinging breasty mount. But there was no one he could turn to now. No one at all.

Low voices sounded outside the door. He tried not to listen to them. He knew what was going on. Ben Montereale was making a deal with the reporters. Not every Hollywood scandal got into the papers. The really good lawyers knew how to protect their clients. And Ben was a really good lawyer.

A long time passed. Lyle remained motionless on the couch, trying not to think of anything at all. Finally there came a knock.

"Who's there?"

"It's Ben, Kevin. Let me in."

"Are they gone?"

"Everybody's gone. Open up."

Shakily, Lyle admitted the lawyer. Montereale was sweating profusely, and he had chewed his cigar to a sticky pulp. He spat it out and lit a new one.

"Well?" Lyle said tensely.

Montereale exhaled smoke. "It's all taken care of, about the newspapers."

"There won't be any story?'

"There'll be a story, all right," the lawyer said. "It'll say that young starlet Audrey Reynolds jumped to her death from the hotel suite of Leo Naumann Productions executive Kevin Lyle this evening, while discussing the part she would play in a forthcoming Naumann production. The story will go on to say that Miss Reynolds had been in a bad nervous state for some time. End of story. It'll be a squib someplace on page twenty of the morning editions, instead of being an eight-column streamer in the late papers tonight."

"Did my name have to be mentioneed?" Lyle asked.

"There wasn't any way out of it. Some of them promised to downplay the story, maybe even to cut you out of it completely. But they couldn't be sure. The fact still remains that it'll be a very unsensational story. No mention of her having been drunk, no mention of her having been Leo Naumann's mistress. The way it'll look to the pubic, it'll be just another hopped-up starlet getting a fit of despondency and leaping out a window while in the middle of a conference concerning the future of her career. Not a bedroom story at all. I think you'll come out of it okay."

"But can you be *sure?*" Lyle wanted to know. "Suppose they doublecross you?"

"They won't."

"Just suppose. Suppose one of those guys who you talked to out there was a guy looking for a raise, or something. And he goes home and tells his city editor that here's a big story, and everybody else is going to play it down, but if they play it up they'll have a scoop."

Montereale shook his head doggedly. "It won't happen. Kevin, I play right along with these guys. Not only the reporters but the city editors, too. You got to remember my position. I'm at the center of half the scandal and adultery and fornication in this town. I'm a prime news source. When it suits me, I give out information. When it suits me, I suppress it. Any city editor who displeases me will have to get his Ben Montereale news from the other newspapers, not from me, and they all know it damn well. The story's squashed. Your nose will stay clean at least for this time."

"Jesus, Ben, I can't thank you enough. I thought for sure I'd be hauled off to jail on this thing."

Montereale shrugged. "You're lucky, that's all. But your luck won't hold out forever. Something like what happened tonight wasn't your fault, but it doesn't look good all the same. Just make sure you don't get into any more scrapes, that's all I have to tell you. We'll be ready to go to court in not too many more weeks. I think I've got a solid case against Donna now. But don't go messing things up by getting into a lot of harebrained crap. Just live a nice orderly life and stay out of trouble."

"I try, Ben. I can't help it if some hot-pants girl had to come pick my window to —"

"Did you really just meet that girl last night, Kevin?"

"What? Why, yes. Yes, sure. And —"

"And you laid her, didn't you. Last night. At Naumann's place. That's why she came to you. She figured you'd help her."

"Christ, Ben, how can you say a thing like that?'

Montereale's eyes blazed angrily. "Don't lie to me, Kevin. I can see right through you."

Lyle sighed. "Okay, your honor. I admit it. I

slept with the Reynolds girl last night. Are you a mindreader, or do you have a spy planted at Naumann's mansion?"

"Neither," Montereale said frostily. "I've just been around long enough to read between the lines. You were hot, and you probably got a chance to tear off a quick one while Naumann was busy with this other woman. Then later on Naumann gave the Reynolds the heave, and she came on over here figuring you were ripe for a new steady piece. You weren't anxious, even after she did strip, so she got heated up and jumped. Probably regretted it the moment she went overboard."

"You give me the creeps," Lyle said. "That's almost exactly what happened "

"So you're out grabbing easy stuff," Montereale said. He shook his head solemnly. "I knew you couldn't stay a hermit. But at least be more subtle about it. Pick up a tramp floozie and get your ten bucks' worth. Don't get involved in complicated situations like this. They only get you in trouble. And then I have to get you out of trouble, and I miss my dinners and get sore."

"I wish I could make it up to you for the inconvenience of this evening, Ben."

"Don't worry. It'll be on your bill in the end." Montereale moved toward the door. "Just play it a little smarter, Kevin. I can't keep on bailing you out."

"Thanks for everything," Lyle said.

The door closed.

Don Elliott

Lyle was alone.

He looked at his watch. Almost nine o'clock. Practically three hours of confusion. Now things were quiet again.

He remembered he hadn't eaten dinner. He felt hollow inside, but the thought of food sickened him. There was still the sour taste of vomit in his mouth, and his head throbbed mercilessly. And he was alone now, absolutely alone. No one to turn to. Not a friend to go to. His loins ached with desire. His brain pounded painfully

I need a drink, he decided.

CHAPTER TEN

MAKING AN EFFORT, HE PULLED himself together, combed his hair, straightened his clothes. Then, with what he hoped was complete dignity and self-possession, he locked his room, walked down the hall to the elevator, and pressed the button. He watched the green lights on the floor indicator go on and off as the elevator rose.

The elevator boy gave him a curious stare as he entered. Lyle felt acutely uncomfortable. He had a brand new notoriety around the hotel that would set tongues wagging every time he made an appearance. He wondered if Williams would ask him to move out. Maybe not; but this wasn't the sort of hotel that relished flashy publicity. It's big selling point was class and dignity. They might not want to keep on renting a suite to the sort of man out of whose windows naked starlets tended to jump. *Screw them*, Lyle thought tiredly. *If they ask me to move out I'll say no. I wasn't responsible for what happened. At least not directly responsible.*

He drew funny stares in the lobby, too. As a result, he changed his idea about having a few drinks in the hotel cocktail lounge and then going to sleep. He didn't want to hang around the hotel tonight. Let things die down a little first.

He walked on through the lobby and out front. His car was parked half a block from the hotel entrance, and, without any clear idea of where he was going, he got behind the wheel and began to drive. He had gone about seven blocks eastward when a neon bar sign impinged on his consciousness, and almost automatically he slowed the car to a halt and slid frontwards into a parking spot. He switched the car off and got out, thumbing his eyeballs for a moment before going into the bar.

It was a bigger place than it seemed from the outside, long and dim, with elaborate modernistic fixtures and a fancy decor. Lyle slid heavily into a vacant booth near the back. Soft music filtered out of speakers over his head. Lush, dreamy music, with thick violin melodies. He closed his eyes and listened for a moment.

Then he realized a waiter had come over and was trying to take his order. He looked up, embarrassed.

"Dry martini," he said without much thought.

"Martini, yes. Olive or lemon peel?"

He shrugged. "Olive, I guess. I don't care. Just make it good and strong."

Mistress of Sin

The waiter, a good-looking Latin type, smiled knowingly and glided away. Lyle closed his eyes again. Over the music came the sound of a cocktail shaker in operation. Then the sound of a drink being put down on his table. He opened his eyes and looked at the drink. Crystal clear, with little beads of sweat on the outside of the glass. A shallow glass; California martinis ran small and low-priced. For half a dollar, you got a couple of ounces of martini; in New York you'd pay seventy or eighty cents, maybe more, but you'd get a proportionally heftier drink. Lyle picked the glass up, contemplated it gravely for an instant, and took a sip. It was cold. It was potent. That was all he asked.

He wasn't much of a martini drinker. They went to his head fast, and they bothered him the next day, and ordinarily he avoided them. But right now the cold martini seemed almost magically satisfying. He took two more dainty sips, then gulped the rest down in a hurry. There was a rewardingly warm glow inside him almost immediately.

But the glow was phony, he knew. It wore off, leaving you no better off than you were before, just a little lighter in the pocket. Getting cheerful by drinking was like keeping company with a girl who wore a padded bra. It was okay to sit here feeling the cozy glow of alcohol, just as it was okay to look at the girl's agreeably swollen sweater. But the reckoning always comes. Reality always sticks in its oar. The moment arrives when you don't have a boozy glow any more, just a hangover. And the moment arrives when you get the sweater off the girl, and you get the falsies off her too, and you find out that underneath those big exciting curves in that tight sweater there was nothing but a lot of foam rubber and a pair of very small skimpy breasts.

He shook his head. You can't ever get anywhere by fooling yourself, he thought. There's always that sour taste in your mouth after the night of hitting the bottle. There's always that miserable feeling as you put your hands over that pair of nubby little points that you thought would be great warm firm heaving mounds of heavy woman-flesh.

"Another martini, sir?"

"All right," Lyle said.

It arrived with magic-carpet swiftness. He took his time over it, now. He was starting to get into a reflective, almost philosophical mood.

A girl was dead. A girl he hardly knew at all. He had made love to her twenty-four hours ago, that was all. Had sprawled on top of her, had held her breasts in his hands — no skimp phony points on Audrey — had thrust himself into her warm waiting woman-ness.

For two seconds, at least, it hadn't been two bored, unhappy people having a casual lay. It had been Romeo and Juliet, Tristan and Isolde, Paolo and Francesca. For that one long pounding instant when two joined bodies throbbed and quivered with the same jolt of electricity running through them, all the tinsel unrealities dropped away and the only thing that counted was the physical excitement.

Well, they had had that. And now she was dead, a broken mess of bones, the pretty face a horrifying ruin, the delicate little nose squashed flat, the white teeth splintered, the laughing eyes so much dead jelly, the full breasts flat-tened and crushed.

What for? he asked himself.

What the hell for?

Because she was disappointed. She had lost the love of Leo Naumann and she had lost her big movie chance, and after that she saw no rea-son why she should not lose life as well. Arro-gant of her, really. To throw her only life away in a fit of pique. How old was she? Twenty? Twenty-two? Ten or fifteen years ahead of her beauty. Twenty, maybe, during which she would have been desirable to many men. She could have had a fine career. A good life. Vacations in Mexico, a powder-blue Cadillac, handsome lov-ers, a weekly fifty-dollar rubdown by a homo-sexual masseuse who would knead the curves of her breasts and buttocks with impersonal fi-nesse. And she had tossed it all away. Tossed it all out the window.

He finished the second martini.

His head was starting to get foggy, now. He hadn't eaten dinner, had hardly eaten lunch just a sandwich at his desk — and even the sand-wich wasn't inside him any more, not since he had thrown up. With precision, Lyle plucked the olive out of his empty glass and gobbled it up.

He didn't need to look around for the waiter. The man was at his elbow almost immediately to remove the glass.

"Will it be another?"

"In a little while," Lyle said, his voice growing thick. "I'll let you know when I'm ready."

"Of course, sir."

Lyle leaned forward, propping his head on his hands. He thought about Lorayne. She was with Leo Naumann at this very moment, most likely. In his Amatorium. Christ only knew what weird stunt they were up to. Naumann might be laced up tight in one of his corsets, and Lorayne wearing one of his special outfits that covered her entire body except for her buttocks. And she would be kneeling over, presenting those two delectable pink cheeks to Naumann's whip. He wouldn't hit her hard, oh, no! Just hard enough to bring color to her buttocks and excitement to his loins.

Lyle wondered what other quaint old-world perversion Naumann might introduce Lorayne to. His script-writer's mind quickly brought the scene to life in three dimensions. Lorayne, naked, spread-eagled on a table, arms and legs bound to the sides of the table. Naumann pretending to be a torturer, capering around her, then climbing on top of her and violating her as she lay trussed with her legs apart. Naumann wasn't satisfied to take his sex the ordinary way. He had to play a little game, make a little perverted drama out of it.

Or a third possibility. Lorayne dressed in a

black leotard with holes cut to bare her breasts and buttocks. Naumann stark naked, lying on his stomach getting spanked. And rolling over to spank Lorayne in turn. Squeezing her lovely breasts, biting them maybe. And finally the two of them going at it tooth and nail.

Lyle shook his head. He could vividly see the imaginary scenes, and as he pictured each one he felt a little tingle of vicarious desire. He could sense the smooth buttocks and feel the firm flesh grow warm. He could understand the pleasure of being whipped by her. Of taking part in strange practices. Lorayne was the sort of woman who inspired men to do such things. No wonder Naumann was crazy about her.

Why did I let him have her?

He signalled for a third martini.

Why did I bring her to him? What did it gain me, besides a girl's death on my conscience? Am I better off for the raise Naumann gave me? God, what a mess everything is turning into! He took a deep drink.

"Hello," a warm voice said somewhere not more than six inches from his right ear. "Mind if I sit down and keep you company? You look lonely."

He turned. Through blurred eyes he managed to make out the figure of a girl hovering over his booth. No, not a girl, a woman; she was at least thirty, he figured, seeing with sudden clarity the little pouches of flesh under her eyes, the softness at her throat. She was a redhead, well built, wearing an extremely low-cut silk blouse that hung open in front far enough to tell him that she had no bra on. He could see the upper curves of big, very white breasts, and the dark brown buttons of her nipples thrusting against the fabric. Without waiting for an answer, she slipped into the booth at his side, the warmth of her thigh burning against him.

"I'm Jeanie," she said. Her voice was husky. "I hate to see anybody looking as miserable as you do. Buy me a drink and tell me all about it. Get it off your chest."

The waiter came up to them, and Jeanie said smoothly, "Rye and ginger, Tom. And how about another martini for you, eh?"

Lyle shook his head fuddledly and indicated his still unfinished drink. "Not — not just yet."

Part of his mind was still rational enough to tell him that he had wandered into a very expert clip joint and was about to be taken for a very professional ride by this B-girl. But he was too rooted to the spot to object. He said nothing, as the girl's drink arrived.

Jeanie cooed, "What's your name, handsome? I want to be friends with you."

"Gable," he said. "Clark Gable. I'm a movie actor. Maybe you've heard of me."

Her laugh was brittle and phony. "You can't kid me. You're not Clark Gable. He wears a mustache. Maybe you're Jeff Chandler, huh?"

"I'm really Elizabeth Taylor in disguise," he said.

Again the harsh laugh. "Say, you got a real sense of humor when you try! You a comedian?

That would explain why you look so sad. Comedians always look sad except when they got an audience."

He nodded. "Yeah, I'm a comedian."

"What's your name?"

"James Joyce."

"Really?" she asked solemnly.

"James Francis Xavier Joyce, that's me. Honest."

"Sorry to say I never heard of you, Jimmy. You do nightclub work or something?"

"I have a little act, yes," he said. "I do a take-off on the Odyssey. Homer, you know. But I'm out of work right now, you see."

"Sure. That egghead stuff, you can't make a buck in it. That why you look so miserable, Jimmy?"

He shook his head. "Having trouble with my wife." He noticed a new martini had appeared. "Seems she's a lesbian. Been married to her all these years and never knew it. She only sleeps with girls now."

"Jeez. That can really get a fella down. I once knew a girl like that, up in San Fran. Wore her hair short. Real queer duck. Had a quarrel with her girlfriend and jumped out a window."

"I know a girl who jumped out a window, too," Lyle said. He took a deep drink. "Only she wasn't a lesbian. Least I don't think she was."

"You can never tell, Jimmy."

"No. You never can tell."

A second rye-and-ginger replaced Jeanie's empty glass. She took a sip, then moved closer to him. In a low, confidential voice she said. "I like you, Jimmy. You look like a swell guy. I don't want to see you unhappy. You deserve more out of life than you're getting."

"Amen to that."

"I can give you a good time," she went on. "To sort of cheer you up. Don't get me wrong, I ain't a tramp. Just a girl with a good heart. I don't do this sort of thing for everybody." She took his arm, which dangled limply, and draped it over her shoulder. She tugged on the hand until she had pulled it down to the opening of her blouse, and stuffed it inside cupping it over one big breast. He started to pull away, but she said, "Go on, take a feel. It's dark in here, nobody's looking. I got a nice figure, huh? I used to pose for the pictures in the girlie magazines." He remained passive, too drunk to care much about what was going on. The warmth of her breast was pleasant against his palm. It was a huge breast, soft and good to feel.

Taking his other hand, now, she put it on her knee, then lifted her dress. His hand touched her thighs. She had no underwear on, and he felt the heat of her belly, the softness of her thighs. She shifted her hips, putting him in a better position, and at the same time slipped her left hand into his lap. "I got a little room in back we could go to. Okay, Jimmy? Just you and me, and I'll show you a couple tricks I bet you never heard of before. How about?"

"No." He got his hand out from between her legs, and took hers from his.

"N·O. No," he repeated.

She pouted. "You're just saying that, Jimmy. But you really want to do it. Deep down inside, you do."

"No I do not," he said with exaggerated care- fulness. "Now go away and stop bothering me."

Her answer was to dive for him again. He shook her away and called out, "Waiter! Waiter!"

He was on the spot at once. "Another mar- tini, sir?"

"No. Just bring me my check."

"Certainly, sir."

Jeanie threw him a sour look and backed out of the booth. Lyle waited, his head spinning, and a moment later the waiter put a card face down on the table. He turned it over. Five dollars. Pretty steep for four skimpy martinis and a couple of rye-and-gingers that probably didn't have any rye in them. He fumbled through his wallet, found a five and a one, looked at them carefully to make sure that they were not fifties or tens, and put them down. He started to put his wallet away, then took it out again and looked at the bills. Nestling between two singles was Naumann's thousand-dollar bill. Lyle glow- ered at it bitterly. It would have been amusing to hand it to the waiter and wait for change. But, he thought, I'm too drunk to count change now.

He walked unsteadily out.

Pausing for a moment in front of the bar, he drew in several deep breaths and waited for his head to clear. Nothing appreciable happened, but after a moment he got into the car anyway. On the third try, he put the key into the ignition slot. Then he sat behind the wheel a long instant, trying to collect himself. He felt dizzy, hungry, drunk, depressed. The B-girl's professional caresses had reawakened desire in him, and he contemplated that for a moment. He wondered why he had been so rude to the girl. For ten bucks he could have gone into the back room, climbed between her obliging thighs, squeezed her soft white breasts, and rammed away for a couple of minutes, until the instant of pleasure temporarily eased the heartache he felt.

No. Not a B-girl in a back room. That was blasphemy, he thought. Blasphemy against the sacred nature of sex. He didn't want that. He wanted —

He wanted —

What the hell do I want? he wondered.

He stared at his dashboard. *Best thing it just to go home*, he decided. *Let's see, now —*

He regarded the car as though he had never driven one before. Turn the key. That's right. Now step on the gas and press the button. Careful, now, don't roar that engine. This car costs more than a lot of people ever earn in two years. Release the handbrake now. Put the car into first. Get that clutch down, Kevin. Now let it up. Slowly. Feed a little gas. What do you know? It moves.

He rolled away from the curb and came to a

stalled halt a couple of yards further on. Shaking his head, he started to go through the whole
process again. *You shouldn't be driving like this*,
the rational part of his mind told him. *You want
to kill yourself, you damned fool?*

He didn't listen. He had driven before when
drunk, he reminded himself, and he had never
been in an accident in his life. He was a very
good driver. Besides, it didn't matter much
whether or not he did kill himself. He didn't
serve any useful purpose in the world any more.
He had ceased to be a husband to his wife, a father to his children. They were already drifting
away from him. He had sojourned in the world
for thirty-six years, he had sired a son to replace
him in the general scheme of things, and now it
didn't really matter much if he smashed himself
to bits in an auto wreck. He would be small loss
to humanity. Unmourned. He had a useless job
in a trivial industry. It wouldn't be as though a
great poet were dying, he thought. Or a states-
man of a philosopher. It was just Kevin Lyle,
who had had, all things considered, a pretty full
life, and who was scandalously overpaid to help
provide pap and drivel for the great American
mass audience. So it would be nothing very important for him to drive into a lamp-post and
finish himself off.

Automatically, he shifted gears upward,
stopped obediently at the red lights, and in all
ways acted as a competent and sober driver. He
moved mechanically. Getting home was the all-
important goal in his mind, now. Getting home

and getting a good night's rest. He drove on and on, through streets familiar through many years, and the rush of the night air cleared his mind, though he was still a long way from being sober. At length he pulled up in a familiar street in front of a familiar house.

Home at last, he thought, getting out of the car.

Then he stopped. blinked, looked around.

What have I done? Where have I gone?

It had been only a few blocks from the bar back to the hotel. But he had driven for miles and miles.

He was in Pasadena now.

He had gone home, all right.

Home to Donna.

CHAPTER ELEVEN

L YLE WAS JUST SOBER ENOUGH to feel a sense of real panic at his mistake. He wanted to turn and flee, to get away from this place where he no longer belonged. But the thought of driving all the way back to the hotel appalled him. It seemed like an endless trip, and he would be putting his life in the hands of fate with every revolution of the motor. On the way here, he had been too drunk really to care what happened to him. But now he was sobering slightly, enough to be cautious without being really capable of handling the car. He was in that inbetween state that can be more dangerous than total drunkeness. He was afraid to risk the homeward trip.

And, he thought, this was still his home. He had every right to spend a night under his own roof. Donna couldn't force him to risk his life going back. He could sleep in the guest room, as he had done during those last few hellish days before the final break.

There was another point. His fuddled mind served up Donna's words to him with perfect clarity. *"Maybe it isn't too late to put things back together again, Kevin. Not so much for us as for them. We owe them a decent home. And maybe — maybe we could learn to be good to each other too —"*

At any time, he hadn't believed that she was trying to do anything other than seduce him into an indiscretion that could be used against him at the trial. But perhaps not, he thought fuzzily, now. Perhaps she really meant it. It would solve a lot of things to patch up this separation. His whole life had turned into a tightrope act since he and Donna had broken up. *Forgive and forget*, he thought. *A new start. That's what we both need.*

He weaved unsteadily up the walk toward the front door.

The house was dark. Well, Donna had always liked going to bed early. The kids were up at the crack of dawn, and there was little hope of sleep once they got up. Lyle wondered, though: had she gone to bed alone? Or was her lover with her? That greasy bastard Caldwell.

He leaned on the bell.

The chimes made their soft sound within. He waited, and nearly a minute passed, and no one came to the door. Frowning, Lyle rang again. He tried to see through the double thickness of doors, the wooden one and the screen one. Another long wait. Then, just as he put his thumb on the button for the third time, he saw the viewer-latch in the outer door swing upward.

An eye peered outward.

Donna said, "Who is it — Kevin?"

"Give that little lady sixty-four dollars."

"What do you want? Do you realize it's after eleven o'clock at night?"

"I came for a visit."

"It's only Tuesday. And you're supposed to come in the mornings, not in the middle of the night. Do you think the children are still up at this hour?"

"I didn't come to see them. I came to see you."

"*Me?*"

"Please open the door, Donna."

"You're drunk, that's what you are! Go away! Get out of here or I'll call a cop!"

Very tiredly he said, "I've come a long way, and I'm not in any shape to drive back to my hotel tonight. Please let me in. I'll stay in the guest room. In the morning I'll visit with the kids for a little while and then I'll go away. I won't bother anybody."

"You can't stay here overnight."

"Why the hell not? This is still my house! I paid for it. My sweat. My hard work. You didn't do a thing. And now I show up at my own home, sick and exhausted, and you won't even let me in. I —"

"Be quiet, Kevin. You're shouting. You can be heard all over Pasadena."

"Then let me in."

"No. You're drunk. God only knows what you'll do once I open this door."

He forced his voice down to a temperate level. "I promise you, Donna, that I'll behave myself with the utmost — the utmost — I'll behave properly."

"I don't trust you."

"What the hell do you think I am, a murderer? Come on, let me in. I know why you're keeping me out here. It's because Caldwell is in there with you."

"Don't be an ass."

"He is, isn't he? And you're afraid I've got a gun and I'll shoot him and you both and get possession of the kids. Well, it isn't a bad idea, but I'm not going to do it. Just let me come in and go to bed. I don't give a damn what you and Caldwell do. Just keep your door closed so I don't have to hear anything."

"He isn't here, Kevin."

"Then why don't you let me in?" To his surprise, he found tears welling up in his eyes, and the next moment he was hanging unsteadily to the doorknob and blubbering like a baby. "God damn it, Donna," he said between sobs, "why do you have to keep me out here like this? I'm in no shape to go home. I've got to stay here."

There was silence from within. As he fought to get control over himself, Lyle thought, *I've really screwed things up now. Shouting and ranting like this. All Donna needs to do is get a couple of the neighbors to testify that I came around late at night drunk and disorderly to demand entry and I'll be cooked in court.*

He considered going around back and curling up in the yard until morning. He considered getting into his car and risking the drive back. He considered pounding on the door some more.

He said quietly. "Donna. please let me in."

"All right, Kevin." she said surprisingly.

Lyle waited as she unchained the door and pulled it open. He stepped in, walking heavily and with great care. He was afraid of tripping over his own feet and plunging drunkenly to the floor.

"Much obliged," he said.

She was wearing only a filmy housecoat. Donna had always slept nude, and he could see that she was nude now beneath the light wrap. It was open at the throat. revealing the upper swells of her lovely breasts. Her hair was up in curlers, her face glossy with cold-cream, but even those domestic touches failed to destroy her body's appeal.

"Come into the kitchen," she said quietly. "I'll put up some black coffee for you." She sounded genuinely concerned about him. "What did you do, go out on a bender tonight and then drive all the way here?"

"That's about it."

"I thought you had more sense than that, Kevin."

"So did I. It was a rough day, though." He cut himself short just as he was on the verge of telling her about the suicide of Audrey Reynolds. Somewhere in the blurred haziness of his mind, a cold, incisive voice whispered, *Remember that you're engaged in a legal battle with this woman who used to be your wife. She's friendly now, but it might be a trick. Remember that anything you say or do can be used against you in the custody fight.*

As she moved around the kitchen, getting the coffeepot out of the cupboard and turning on the stove, he said, "Did I wake you up?"

"I went to bed ten minutes ago. I hadn't really fallen asleep yet."

"It was a big surprise to me to find myself here. I just got into the car and drove, and I guess my unconscious reflexes did the rest." *A fine thing to tell her,* the sober part of his mind carped. *You expect to win custody of those kids admitting that you were so drunk you didn't know where you were going?*

"You ought to be more careful, Kevin. Those freeways are dangerous enough when you're sober."

"That's why I had to ask you to let me stay here. I'm afraid of driving home while I'm — like this."

"You sound pretty sober now."

"I'm coming out of it. But I'd hate to drive now."

She put a steaming cup of coffee in front of him. As she did so, the front of her gown dropped open, and he caught a glimpse of twin rounded whitenesses. With an automatic modest gesture, she closed the gown up again, but not before a pang of lust had gone through

Lyles' body. He remembered in pain the many times he had fondled those breasts, had kissed the hard little nipples, had billowed his head between the two soft fleshy bulks.

Donna straightened up. "Here. Drink this. It'll do you some good. I'll go make up the guest room for you."

"No — wait — stay here —"

She frowned at him. "It's getting late, Kevin. The children wake me up so early. What is it?"

"I — just want you to stay here —"

"I told you, it's getting late —"

"And you want to get back upstairs to Caldwell?"

Anger flamed in her face. "That was a stinking thing to say! I ought to make you get out?"

"Well? Is he up there? Hiding under the bed or something?"

"Do you want to search the house?" Donna asked acidly. "I'll give you a flashlight and a broom and you can go poking into the closets. How about it?"

He shook his head morosely. "Forget it."

"No. You're convinced that Bruce is hiding here somewhere. and I want you to see for yourself. Bruce isn't the type to hide. If he were here, he'd come out and not be afraid. But he doesn't stay the night here."

"I believe you," he said irritably.

But she wouldn't let the subject drop. "There's no reason for me to deny that I plan to marry Bruce as soon as it's legally possible. He's mature and considerate and well established

professionally, and the children like him. But I
don't engage in anything immoral. You'll never
find him here at night, no matter how hard you
look."

Lyle snickered. "You indulged in plenty that
was immoral before you married me. Remember? Hopping into bed with me every chance you
got, while waiting for your divorcee from what's-
his-name to come through?"

"That was different," she said. "Don't get me
wrong. I don't think a marriage license is neces-
sary before two people who love each other can
go to bed with each other. But there are children
in the house now. I've got to think of them, of
their developing personalities, their adjust-
ments. What would they think if they woke up
one morning and found that Bruce had slept
over? Or if they came into the bedroom in the
middle of the night and found Bruce with me?
Uh-uh. The transition from one daddy to another has to be made carefully."

"Caldwell isn't ever going to be daddy to
those kids. He'll just be your husband."

"Stepdaddy, then. The fact remains that he'll
be important to them. He'll be the man they see
most often."

"I know. That's what hurts so goddam
much." He looked up at her, eyes full of pain.
"Donna — tell me when did things start going
off the track? Why did all this have to happen in
the first place?"

"It's too late to ask things like that now"

"But it didn't need to happen. Did it? Other

people in this crazy town stay married twenty, thirty, forty years. Why did we break up?"

She shook her head. "The reasons don't matter any more. We just — drifted apart, that was all. Until we were living in different worlds. I guess I was bored, Kevin. Heck, you gave me everything I wanted — maybe that was the trouble. I still like you. I always will. But there was just one morning when I woke up and realized that I couldn't go on being your wife any longer."

She was twisting things, distorting them, he told himself wearily. It was her boredom, her selfishness that had driven her to take lovers. And his sense of outrage that had broken things up. She was perfectly willing to go on being his wife indefinitely — on her terms, which meant unlimited sex freedom for her. He couldn't abide that. But somehow she had shifted the blame to make it seem that it was his dullness rather than her amorality that had ruined their marriage. *Maybe a little of both*, he thought. *But 1 tried. Christ, 1 tried.*

He gulped down his coffee.

"Want some more?" Donna asked.

"No. I won't be able to fall asleep tonight."

"Come on. I'll put you up now. The kids will be startled to see you at breakfast."

"I'll bet they will."

He rose heavily and followed her through the darkened house to the guest room. There was a folding couch in there that opened into a double bed. He tugged it open for her, then stepped

Don Elliott

back while she put the sheets and pillow on it. Then she was done, he sat down on the edge of the bed and put his head in his hands.

A dry sob escaped his lips. "This is the worst thing of all," he muttered.

"What is?"

"Being a guest in my own home."

"It's the only way we can work it now," Donna said.

They were silent for a moment. Through Lyle's mind passed the events of the day. The naked girl posturing and prancing in his room. Leaping from the window. Then the inquisition, the reporters, all that turmoil. And then the drinking. The B-Girl with her hand between his legs. His hand holding a fleshy breast. And Lorayne belonging to Leo Naumann.

Fierce sexual desire sizzled inside him.

He remembered other things. Donna lying in a field, stark naked, her young breasts rising and falling steeply in the excitement after their first lovemaking. Donna in a bikini on the beach at Cannes, on their honeymoon. Donna warm and moist and naked and panting in bed, night after night after night. Donna tanned and radiant, clinging to him with savage abandon.

Donna —

He looked up at her. "Donna —" He paused, moistening his lips. "Donna, come close for a moment —"

She sat down on the bed next to him. Tension tingled in the air. Neither of them moved for a long moment.

Then she said, "I've been so lonely, Kevin."

"So have I."

"Rolling around in the bed — on fire — the day you were here, last Sunday, and we started to make love and you got angry and threw me off your lap — I was sick all that day. Sick with heartache. And I ached down here, too." She took his hand, opened her gown, placed it lightly on the fleece at her loins. He didn't move it. He knew what was going to happen, now. The same thing as on the last visit. Donna was hungry for sex. And he happened to be handy.

He couldn't resist.

He drove his hand into her body with sudden intensity, and she gasped in delight and pulled off her gown, and there she was, naked next to him, her body still young, bursting with sexual vitality. She clamped her warm thighs tight together over his hand and began to stroke his body.

He lost control. Springing up, he tossed off his clothing with abandon and let her drag him down onto the bed once again. Her body was alive against him, the ripe hills of her breasts bobbing and swaying, the nipples growing erect, her legs parting to receive him.

Their bodies joined.

Now it was an old, well-rehearsed pattern. They had done it together how many times? Hundreds. Seven years, more or less, and it had been every night at the beginning, then at least three or four times a week even after the children came. They had performed this act thousands of times. Their supple bodies moved with an ease born of long practice. Every quiver, every ripple of a muscle, every squeeze, every intake of breath had its own particular meaning. Body thrust against body; sweat mingled with sweat. saliva with saliva.

All thoughts of Lorayne left his mind, all thoughts of the divorce squabble, of the dead girl who had plunged from his window, of the fleshy B-girl in the bar. The only thing that had reality in the world was this action going on now, the two people writhing on the groaning bed.

"Kevin . . . . *Kevin*," she whimpered.

"Lover . . . ."

"Deeper," she murmured. "Yes, that's it — like that — again and again and again and — oh — oh oh oh — oooohhhh — *Kevin!*"

The sounds poured in a torrent from her lips as she moved frantically beneath him. He felt her quiver and throb as she reached a climax, then after a moment of pause return to the struggle. A second time and a third she mounted the heights of excitement, heaving, rearing, thighs locked tight around him.

"Ah — yes — yes, that's it — now, Kevin! Eve-rything you've got! Ev-e-r-y-thing you've got —"

Her voice died into a low moaning scund, but words were no longer needed now. He understood what she was feeling, smelled the musky passion-smell of completion, and with a series of powerful thrusts that sent rippling eddies of pleasure up as far as his shoulder-blades he exhausted his passion on her trembling body.

He held tight as the last shudder of delight went through him. He was calm, now, the instant it was over. The fit of passion had passed. So had the last lingering vestiges of his drunkenness.

Christ almighty, he thought. *Now I've done it. Come bursting in here drunk as a lord and let her trap me into going for a ride on her. The scheming little bitch.*

He tried to pull free. but she clasped her arms around his back and held him tight.

"Stay here, Kevin."

"Let go."

"No. I want you. Stay here all night and do it to me again and again. Like we did when we first knew each other. Remember the night when we did it five times? We were so proud of ourselves. Let's do it that way again . . . ."

"I've got to leave."

"Don't be silly, Kevin. It must be midnight or later. And you said you couldn't drive home."

"I'm sober now." Inexorably, he wrenched free of her grasp. She lay naked on the bed, looking at him with big-eyed innocence. He forced himself to ignore the temptation of her high, pointed breasts and beckoning thighs. She was a witch, a temptress, a Delilah. But he had to get away from her. Next thing he knew, she would be whispering reconciliation into his ear, and there would be no divorce, no custody fight, and everything would go on as it had been going on, with a succession of lovers keeping her warm in the daytime while he sweated to pay for her minks and her vacation trips.

He began to dress.

"I can't understand you, Kevin. You cry like a two-year-old when I lock you out. Then I let you in and you make love to me and run away."

"I can't stay here. I should never have even come here in the first place."

She rose and pressed herself against him, the tips of her breasts grazing his shirt. "You're upset, Kevin," she crooned. "You've been through so much, and now you're so confused you don't know what you want. Stay here. Get a good night's sleep. Tomorrow we can talk things over, figure it all out. Maybe we can stay together after all. Maybe —"

"No!" he roared. Breaking loose from her, he jammed his feet into his loafers, slipped into his clothes, and made his way to the door.

"Kevin! Kevin, come back!"

"Leave me alone," he muttered. He turned, caught a last glimpse of her, naked, her breasts moving rapidly, her nipples still stiff with desire, her arms outstretched in appeal. He scowled and plunged out the door and into the night.

CHAPTER TWELVE

HE STARTED THE CAR AND DROVE away at twelve miles an hour, hands tight to the wheel. Dark, silent houses flowed past; occasionally a bright house, where a party was going on. Lyle felt cold and bitter. Coming to the house had been a stupid blunder, he thought. But staying there — putting himself at Donna's mercy had been worse than stupid. It had been criminally foolish.

Now everything was irreparably screwed up, he told himself as he inched gingerly onto the freeway and carefully moved into the outside lane, where the sparse night traffic was travelling at a relatively slow pace. He shuddered at the prospect of having to tell Ben Montereale that, the same night as the Audrey Reynolds suicide, he had gotten drunk and gone to see his wife and had let her seduce him. Or had seduced her. It had been a mutual seduction, but Donna would be able to make more capital out of it than he would. Separated people weren't supposed to sneak back together for a quick roll in the hay while nobody was looking. It damaged his entire case to be shown sexually dependant in this way. And Donna knew it. She wouldn't miss a trick in her battle for the kids.

Montereale would flay him. He might even drop the case. Everything was jeopardized now, and Ben liked to be a winner. His reputation depended on it. He wouldn't want to remain involved in a case where his client methodically got tangled in one scrape after another, as though determined to hand the advantage to the opposition.

Some people are accident prone, Lyle thought. *I guess I'm accident prone*. It had certainly been a hectic few days, since the moment Saturday afternoon when he had stopped for a red light and picked up a pretty hitchhiker.

Was it only four days? It seemed like ages. But how few hours had passed, and how much had happened. Saturday, Sunday, Monday, now Tuesday. Tuesday was over, Wednesday was in its first hour. And so much had happened.

One cockeyed thing after another. The fight with the drunk at the nightclub. The torrid session with Lorayne on the dressing-room floor, mingling blood and sweat. The swimming excursion. Introducing Lorayne to Naumann. Going to bed with Audrey. Then Audrey's suicide. The martinis in the bar, the B-Girl, the drunken wrong-direction drive.

And the session with Donna.

Event had followed event with incredible rapidity. Lyle felt dazed by it all. He was a man caught up in a whirlwind of turmoil. He could no longer see his way clear. He was shrouded in bewilderment.

A horn honked angrily behind him. He glanced down at his speedometer, saw that he was doing only thirty. A car cut out behind him and came zooming up on his right; the driver yelled something obscene at him and sped off into the darkness. Lyle touched the gas pedal a little more heavily. He was no longer worried about getting into an accident. Donna's coffee had done its job. But he hardly cared whether he got home alive or not.

It was past one in the morning by the time he pulled into a waiting parking lot in front of his hotel. The night desk man gave him a peculiar stare as he walked in; obviously the suicide story had gotten around. Someone had left a copy of the late edition of the *Herald & Express* lying on one of the lobby couches. Lyle picked the paper up, uncrumpled it, and with a sense of impending disaster began to look over the front-page headlines.

The big spread shrieked, DODGERS BELT BRAVES TWICE, 3-1, 9-7. A secondary headline announced, COPTER CRASH IN SANTA MONICA KILLS FOUR. Smaller stories concerned Russian threats at the U.N., a selling splurge on the New York Stock Exchange, and a statement from the President about the unemployment problem on the West Coast. Nothing about any starlets having jumped naked from anybody's windows.

Lyle turned the page. Nothing on page two. Nothing on page three. Nothing on page four.

Five. Six. Seven. Was this too early an edition? The suicide had happened at six o'clock. The reporters hadn't arrived till nearly seven. What time did this edition come out? Nine? Ten? Maybe they hadn't had time to get the story into print. Maybe it would be splashed all over tomorrow's morning editions.

Then he found it. A box on the bottom of the nineteenth page. The story was two paragraphs long. Just the bare statement of the events, not even mentioning his name. "The apartment of an executive assistant to Leo Naumann," was the way it was phrased. That was a relief. Montereale's influence had been effective, then. Lyle stuffed the newspaper into a corner of the couch and walked toward the elevator.

He rode upstairs in silence. The night elevator man rarely spoke to anybody, and for once Lyle was grateful for his taciturnity.

Lyle let himself into his room and caught a quick glimpse of himself in the mirror. Eyes red and haggard, cheeks puffy, forehead wrinkled. He looked like a wreck. Kicking off his shoes, he lowered himself into an armchair, sat there for about five minutes with a blank mind, then undressed, got into bed, and was asleep almost immediately. He hadn't bothered to set any alarms.

But an alarm rang all the same. He heard

the bell going off, groped reluctantly to con‑
sciousness, and looked around for the clock. His
finger found the button; it was shoved in. The
clock wasn't making the sound. The bell was
still ringing.

The phone.

Lyle's sleep‑fogged, aching brain began to
function. He reached for the phone, simultane‑
ously coming to the realization that it was
morning, that the night had sped by in one
quick burst.

"Hello?"

"Kevin. I've been trying to reach you all
morning at your office."

"Whozis?"

"Lorayne. Darling, is it all right if I come up?
I've got to see you."

He tried to clear the cobwebs from his mind.
"All right if you come up? Where are you now?"

"Downstairs. In your lobby."

"Eh? And you want to come up," he repeated
fuzzily. "Well —"

"If you're busy, I can come back later."

"No," he said. "Come on up. I guess. Jesus,
I'm still half asleep. What time is it, anyway?"

"Quarter past eleven. I'm on my way."

The phone clicked. Shaking his head, he
dropped the receiver into the cradle, dragged
himself out of bed, and padded across the floor
and into the bathroom. He splashed cold water
in his face until he felt reasonably awakened.
He combed his hair, slipped into a dressing
gown, and shuffled to the door to answer

166

Lorayne's knock.

"Morning," he said. "How can you look so beautiful at such an hour?"

"I've been up a long time," she said. She entered the room with brisk, nervous steps. She was dressed simply, almost demurely, in a rather severe tailored suit. Her usually flamboyant pony-tail was piled up in a bun on the back of her head, further hiding her glamour. She looked troubled. Her eyes, like his, were red-rimmed and circled with dark rings. Nervously, she lit a cigarette. Lyle lowered himself to the edge of the bed and watched her, waiting for some explanation of her visit.

"You don't look so good," he said.

"Neither do you."

"I've got a hangover," he told her. "What's your excuse?"

"Kevin, I — I'm all confused. About everything."

"That makes two of us." He looked at her steadily. "You shouldn't be here. If Leo finds out that you go around paying men visits at home, he'll be furious. With you and with me both."

"Leo's in New York," Lorayne said. "Or rather he's on his way. There's some big hassel with the publisher of the hardcover edition of the Africa book, and he got a call late last night to come to New York and straighten things out. He tried to reach you, but he couldn't find you anywhere, so he went himself. He took a flight around eight this morning, and he's coming back tomorrow if everything's okay."

Lyle digested the long speech and realized he would probably be due for a roasting from Naumann upon the producer's return. Naumann men were always supposed to be available, any hour of the day or night. Lyle said, "Why are you here?"

"I want to stay with you."

"Huh?"

"I can't go on with Leo. He's too much for me. I've got to get away from him."

"After *one night?*"

Lorayne nodded. "It was unbelievable. You know, Monday night, the night you brought me over, Leo made love to me while you were outside. And I knew right then that he was a sick man. But I figured I could put up with him. But last night —" She hesitated. "Kevin, it was like Joe Hammond, all over again only ten times as bad."

"Did he — hurt you?"

"It was insane, Kevin. Corsets and whips and weird positions and all the rest. I went along with it, because he's such a powerful man. When I'm with him I can't resist him. I do anything he wants me to do. But then around half past eleven there was the call from New York. And he was so busy arguing and trying to find you and making plane reservations that he didn't have any time for me. I lay awake, tossing and turning, and *thinking*. About Naumann. And about going on for weeks or months with him and his crazy perversions. And I decided I couldn't take it. That I had made a big mistake ever to get involved with him."

Lyle closed his eyes. They ached furiously, and his tongue seemed to be coated with cotton. After a moment he said hollowly, "Don't be impulsive, Lorayne. Naumann's a queer duck, sure. But stick with him. At least until the movie is made. After that you'll be an established star, you'll be able to make your own way without him."

"I couldn't," she said in a low voice. "He disgusts me."

"He isn't that bad."

"Have *you* ever slept with him?"

"No, but I've slept with you," Lyle said roughly. "I know your own private tastes in sex. They're pretty much like Leo's, I imagine. Come on, admit it: he gives you pleasure, doesn't he? More than any other man you've ever slept with."

"Yes." It was a barely audible whisper.

"Then why leave him?"

"I'm afraid, Kevin. Afraid of what that man unleashes in me. I can see myself being guided by him, right over the hill into complete perversion. And I don't want it." She was shivering now. "I know I did some — unusual things when we were together. I've always realized I wasn't completely normal about sex, that I liked to be hurt while I was doing it, that I liked to hurt people. But I tried to conquer those impulses. Leo encourages me to give them full play. He'll turn me into something filthy. That's why I've got to get away from him!"

"Can't you hold out a few months?"

"No!" She turned a pale, distraught face to- ward him. "I've got to find someone else, Kevin. Someone I can love, someone who loves me. Who can give me some solid ground to anchor to. Not a nest of filthy perversions. This last night I got a good look at myself and where I was heading. I don't want to end up jumping out a window like that poor girl Audrey."

"So you heard about that, did you?"

She nodded. "Jones — the butler — saw it in this morning's paper. Just a little short thing about the suicide. He left the clipping for me when I came down for breakfast around nine. How did it happen, Kevin?"

"She came here right after you called last evening. She was drunk, and very sore at the world because she had been tossed out by Naumann. She was particularly sore at me be- cause I had been instrumental in leading Naumann to a replacement for her. So she tried to seduce me, and when that didn't work she jumped out the window. To spite me, I guess. She was so drunk she didn't know what she was doing."

"How horrible," Lorayne muttered. "But you see, that's what I'm afraid of. Being driven to the wall the way she was. Leo's insidious. He makes a girl completely dependant on him, physically, financially, emotionally. And then he simply throws them away when he loses inter- est in them. That's what he'll do with me."

"He won't lose interest in you."

"Don't be silly. Leo's not constructed for permanent love affairs."

Lyle shrugged. "So you're being realistic about this, is that it?"

"Very realistic. But I don't want to smash everything up. Kevin, how binding is that contract I signed with Leo yesterday? I didn't have anyone look it over."

"It's the standard contract he always uses," Lyle said. "He's got an out. Down in the fine print it says that if the party of the first part, meaning him, and the party of the second part, meaning you fail to reach a complete understanding on all artistic matters, the contract is void. So if he wants to get rid of you, he simply has to notify you in writing that because of disagreements on the artistic level he can't use you in his film. He has to pay you a month' salary, but what's that? Three thousand. Chicken feed compared with what he'll give you if you stick with him."

Lorayne chewed at a lovely lip. "That's what I was afraid of. But if I leave him, do you think there's a chance he might use me in the movie anyway?"

"Not a hope."

"But if I'm better suited for the part than anybody else in Hollywood —"

"That won't matter to Leo. His sex life comes before everything else, even before his films. There are plenty of actresses around who can handle that part competently. Not more than competently, but who needs greatness? Leo will break your contract the day you leave him, and give the part to somebody else who'll play his kind of games."

"You're positive?"

"Two hundred percent."

Lorayne was silent for a moment. Finally she said, "I was hoping there was some way of staying in the film without going on as Leo's mistress."

"It can't be done. That's why I advise you to stick things out. Even if he disgusts you. You'll still be able to break loose from him three or four months from now and by then the film will be so far along that he'll let you complete it. And after that you'll be able to name your own terms with anyone in Hollywood."

She shook her head sadly. "No, Kevin. That's one price I won't pay for fame. I'd rather go back to dancing at the Orientale than spend the next four months as Leo's plaything."

"Can't you make the effort? Girl, be smart! You're throwing away a million-dollar career."

"I don't care," she said obstinately. "I'd be throwing away my life the other way. My soul. I know what I'd be like after three months of Leo. I'd be completely brainwashed into a creature of total perversion. Whatever's still good and decent in me will be killed by then. And what happens the morning I wake up and find out Leo's found a new toy? I get tossed out. Sure, I'll be a famous star then, I'll be able to make films for anybody. But what good is that if I'm also a sick person? If I'm so loathsome inside that I can't face myself in the mirror? Kevin, I don't want to be one of those actresses you hear about, the aging bachelor women of forty or fifty who make a lot of money and spend it all to satisfy unnatural lusts. I don't want to end up that way. I've had a big awakening since you last saw me. I'm not out for gold and glory any more. I'd like to be a top actress, sure. But not if it means turning myself into a monster."

"And if there's no other way?"

"There's got to be. And if there isn't, I'll do without the glory. I'd rather be a happy person. A wife and a mother. *Your* wife, Kevin."

The three words exploded like bombshells in his face. *"My* wife?"

Her eyes were gleaming excitedly; her face was flushed. "Yes! Darling, you know I love you. Ever since the first moment I saw you. I told you so the other day, and I meant it then and still do. You'll be free of that woman soon, free to marry me. Oh, I'm shameless to put it this way, but I want you so much!"

"Do you realize," he said in a deliberately level voice, "what Leo Naumann would do to me if you walked out on him to marry me?"

"He might be annoyed —"

"Annoyed? He'd have apoplexy. He'd fire me on the spot, and then he'd blacklist me all over town. I wouldn't be able to get a job as a filling station attendant, let alone as a movie man."

"He wouldn't."

"You don't know him. Leo thinks of himself as a czar. What happens if someone walks off

with the czar's mistress? Do you think it's toler-
ated?"

"We could manage," Lorayne said.

"It's suicide."

"But I love you," she said. Impulsively, she
sprang across the room at him, wrapping her
arms around him with tigress intensity. Her lips
sought his. He could feel the exciting rounds of
her breasts pressing against him. Her tongue
drove deep within his mouth.

He pulled away. "No, Lorayne. It can't work.
You've got to stick with Leo."

"Never!"

"But this is insane —"

"It isn't!" She flushed, wild. He tried to fight
her back, but she swarmed all over him. She
seized the belt of his dressing gown and untied
it. The gown fell open. She dropped upon him,
and her lips began doing things that sent quiv-
ers of delight through him.

But that same part of his mind that had so
futilely tried to give him advice all week cried
out against the madness of this. Whatever his
feelings for Lorayne, he had to get free of her.
He was jeopardizing his career, his entire life by
letting her sweep him up in her plans. He
couldn't even think of marrying her. He needed
some quiet domestic creature, not a savage
wildcat like this. It was hard to believe that
Lorayne had reformed overnight. She was still
the same smokily passionate creature as ever.
Only now she belonged to Leo Naumann, and
fooling with her was like juggling capsules of

nitroglycerin.

"Lorayne — no, don't —"

She was stripping. She was naked, now, her breasts bursting from the confines of her clothing, her tawny body crawling over his. He made a last futile attempt to protest. Then he gave in to the urgent appeal of her body. He lay back, helpless before the furious onslaught of the girl. His hands went to her breasts, squeezing them, feeling the nipples go rigid. She parted her knees and he gasped as the soft warmth enfolded him, and she began to move, artfully, thrillingly, with evilish skill, and he could no longer worry about what Leo Naumann would say, what Ben Montereale would say, what Donna would say. He gave himself up to her completely, totally, and to hell with the consequences.

CHAPTER THIRTEEN

WHEN IT WAS OVER, A LONG TIME later, sanity returned.

Lyle opened his eyes, propped himself up on one elbow, and looked at her. She lay sprawled out, naked, by his side. Her eyes were shut, but she was awake, her lips curving in a kittenish smile of pleasure. The sight of her full breasts and rounded thighs hit him with the same impact as ever. It was as though each time he looked on her nakedness was the first time all over again.

"Lorayne?"

"What is it, darling?"

He paused. "You've got to go."

Her eyes opened wide. "Go? Where can I go?"

"You can't stay here."

"I've got no place else. I moved out of my old place yesterday. And I don't want to go back to Naumann's except to pick up my things."

"You've got to go back there," Lyle said.

Don Elliott

"How can you say that? Darling, I want to stay with *you*. I don't ever want to see Leo again."

In a hollow voice he said, "I've got to get to the office. It's past noon now. We can discuss your future some other time, Lorayne."

"In other words, go away, little girl, you're bothering me," she said acidly.

"No, that's not it at all."

"Then what? You've told me to clear out. Very very nice. Maybe there's something I'm just getting to understand about you, Kevin. A streak of selfishness, of unwillingness to put yourself out for other people."

"For Christ's sake, Lorayne. I did all I could to help you, didn't I?"

"For your own sake. It would get you in better with Leo to find him a nice new mistress."

"I did it to help you." He looked at her in surprise. "We're quarreling already. Like a couple of old married people."

"I don't mean to be bitchy," Lorayne said. "I'm just asking you to let me stay here. With you."

He shook his head slowly. "I can't do it, Lorayne. Look at it my way. I'm a man trying to get custody of his own children. That means I've got to prove I'm morally fit to rear them. How's it going to look if my wife's lawyer discovers I've been living with some starlet while awaiting the decree? And another thing. If Leo finds out where you're staying, he'll can me. I'll have no job, no family, nothing."

"You'll have me," she said quietly. "Or don't you want me?"

He hesitated, caught between his overwhelming desire for this girl and the guilty knowledge that she was too dangerous to get involved with. He didn't want her to leave, but he couldn't allow her to stay.

After a long moment he said, "Listen, Lorayne, give me a couple of days to work things out, will you? Let me think everything through. I've got to consider the divorce problem, my job, a lot of things. And have a talk with my lawyer about my future. After that I'll be able to figure out which way things are heading."

"And in the meantime I go into cold storage somewhere?"

He took his wallet from the dresser and thumbed through it. Naumann's thousand-dollar bill gleamed up at him; he still hadn't deposited it. He took out five twenty-dollar bills, folded them in half, and offered them to Lorayne. "Here. Go get yourself a hotel room. Not in this hotel. A hotel close by. And just stay there and wait a day or so till I know which way things are moving. Okay?"

She stared bitterly at the money without taking it. "You want to get rid of me. Out of your hair. It's worth a few dollars to rid yourself of a nuisance."

"You're misunderstanding everything," he said.

"I understand perfectly." Her voice was cold. Rising from the bed, she gathered her clothing together with impersonal efficiency. He watched, and it was like a knife churning in his vitals to see her pulling the cups of her bra tight over the magnificent thrusts of her bosom. pulling her panties up around the luxurious fullness of her hips. He said nothing while she dressed.

She put her severe jacket on and walked to the door. "So long, Kevin. Thanks for everything."

"Lorayne —" He paused, troubled and hurt. "Look, call me when you've got a place. Let me know where I can reach you, yes?"

"I'll send you a postcard?

The door slammed.

Lyle let out his breath, long and slow. He had never seen Lorayne angry before, and hoped never to see her that way again. She was cold on the outside, boiling within — like an active volcano about to erupt. He had missed the eruption. But the next man who crossed her path this morning was likely to get a torrent of molten lava in his face.

He wondered what to do about the explosive situation shaping up. Nothing, probably. Except sit tight and await further developments. Life had become all too complicated in the past few days. He thought momentarily of dropping the whole business, cashing in a couple of dozen savings bonds, and taking off for Yucatan or Guatemala or some such place where a man could live quietly and at his ease. Then he shook the idea out of his mind. If nothing else, the children were his bond to civilization. He couldn't just go off into the wilderness, romantic as the idea sounded, and leave them behind forgotten.

He reached for the phone and dialed his office. His secretary answered.

"Oh — good afternoon, Mr. Lyle. Did you enjoy your visit with your children?"

Lyle blinked. He remembered that he had told the girl that he wouldn't be in Wednesday morning because he would be seeing his children. But that visit had gone by the boards. "Ah — well, yes, Ellen," he said vaguely. "Look, I understand Mr. Naumann has gone to New York."

"That's right. He left early this morning."

"He hasn't phoned, has he?"

"His plane won't be landing for another fifteen minutes, Mr. Lyle."

"Of course. Did he leave any messages for me at the office, then?"

"Just a note telling you that he had tried to reach you last night and couldn't. He says he'll talk to you when he gets back."

Lyle forced a grin. "Sounds ominous. What's doing around the office this morning?"

"Not very much of anything. I had a call from that writer, Donovan. He said okay for lunch with you on Friday, and wanted to know if you could get him a copy of the book to begin on."

"I'll take care of it. Anything else?"

"That's about it. I've mimeographed up the synopsis you wrote. Everybody's been grabbing copies, and I guess I'll have to run off some more. Will you be coming in this afternoon, Mr. Lyle?"

"I — don't think so," he said slowly. "It's too late in the day to get much done. And I've got a few things to take care of at this end. See you tomorrow, Ellen."

"Right-o," the girl said cheerily.

Lyle put the phone down and began to dress. The day was running away from him; it was quarter to one already, the minutes racing madly by. He dressed and went downstairs for breakfast. There was a note for him in his mailbox, a phone message from Naumann dated the evening before. Lyle crumpled it and went into the hotel coffee shop.

His stomach felt miserable — it had had nothing inside it for twenty-four hours except four martinis and some black coffee — and he ordered a big breakfast, planning to make a sort of brunch out of it. Melon, pancakes, bacon and scrambled eggs, the works. The melon took the edge off the sour taste in his mouth, and he ate it quickly. But when he turned to the pancakes, he discovered that his appetite had completely disappeared. He swallowed three leaden mouthfuls with effort, pushed the plate away, and told the waitress not to bother bringing the bacon and eggs, but to charge him for them anyway. Then he had two cups of coffee to finish off the meal, and left.

At the hotel newstand, he checked the front pages of the morning papers, just to make sure there were no splashy stories about yesterday's suicide. There were none. In a sudden burst of guilt, he crossed the lobby to the manager's office and knocked.

Mr. Williams appeared, looked momentarily startled, then turned on a professionally sleek smile.

"How do you do, Mr. Lyle."

Lyle nodded uncertainly. He ran his tongue around his lips and said, "I just wanted to tell you — how deeply sorry I am for the unfortunate event yesterday — how sorry I am to have caused the hotel any distress —"

"Why, that's very kind of you, Mr. Lyle. But you mustn't feel apologetic. The girl was obviously unbalanced, after all." He chuckled. "A poor choice of phrase. *Unbalanced.* But you mustn't think we hold you responsible in any way. Your lawyer, Mr. Montereale, explained the situation quite thoroughly, as did the police. We're perfectly satisfied that you were nothing but an innocent bystander. And we hope you'll continue to remain one of our valued tenants."

Lyle nodded distantly. "Glad to hear it," he mumbled.

"And now — Mr. Lyle? Are you feeling well?"

"Fine."

"You look pale. And very tired. Perhaps yesterday's happenings have unsettled you. I could send the hotel doctor to give you a sedative —"

"No — no, please. Thank you. Very kind. But I'm okay. Fine. Tip-top."

He fled. His face felt feverishly hot, his eyes had trouble focussing. *I'm coming apart at the seams*, he thought. *Everything going to pieces all at once.*

He went back to his suite. Kicking off his shoes, he went to his desk, and took down a book from the stack of those waiting to be read. Naumann only made one film a year, sometimes two, and he was already bought up for two or three films ahead, but he never stopped looking for important properties. And any publisher who had a Naumann-type novel on his list made haste to send a set of galleys to Kevin Lyle.

He opened this one and flipped through it, sizing it up quickly. It had to be an ambitious book, it had to have that timely timeless touch, and it had to be a potential best seller. Other-wise Leo wouldn't touch it.

This was a political novel — a 600-page story of the maneuverings behind a Presidential nomination. Theoretically it was set in the fu-ture, dealing with the 1968 election, but Lyle quickly saw that it was a thinly disguised par-able drawn from the recent past. The parties were interchanged, various characters were combined and transposed, but the rough out-lines of real people and real events were visible behind the stage makeup of the book's charac-ters. The author was a maverick congressman from California who had been defeated in the last election despite his party's overwhelming victory. He was a controversial figure, and this was certain to be a controversial book. By the time he had read ten pages of it, Lyle was be-ginning to think that this would be an excellent vehicle for Leo Naumann Productions.

He started to make a few rough computa‐
tions. The African film would be completed in
seven or eight months. Then there was the cir‐
cus film to do. Which meant it wouldn't be pos‐
sible for Naumann to get around to this book till
the year after next, possibly even later. But that
didn't matter. A powerful book didn't die in one
season. And maybe it was a good idea to hold off
and release the film during the fervor of the
1964 Presidential campaign. Leo would have the
jump on the competition once again, getting out
a political film of imposing stature while the
others were left at the post.

Completely absorbed now both in the novel
and in his role as story editor, Lyle read on and
on, forgetting about Lorayne and Donna and
Audrey and Leo Naumann and the other confu‐
sions and problems of the past few days. Only
the ringing of the phone some hours later jolted
him out of his state of concentration.

"Long distance call for Mr. Kevin Lyle," the
operator said. "New York calling. Mr. Leo
Naumann, person‐to‐person."

"Lyle speaking," he said.

"Go ahead, New York," came the operator's
voice.

"Kevin?" Naumann demanded. "Listen,
where the hell were you last night?"

"At my wife's place," Lyle said. "I got back
late. I didn't think you'd be looking for me, or —"

"Well, it doesn't matter now. You weren't
around, so I went to New York myself. I'm at the

publishers. These bastards have been trying to give me a hard time all day about the release date of the film, but I think I've finally got them bulldozed."

"Glad to hear it."

"Yeah. Next thing, have you seen or spoken to Lorayne at all today?"

"I — no. No, I haven't," Lyle said, startled.

"That's swell. That's just dandy. I called the house, and Jones said she wasn't around, that she had gone out around ten this morning and he didn't know where. A hell of a thing. And you don't know where she is either?"

"I'm afraid I don't, Leo."

"God *damn* it." There was a crackling note of violent displeasure in Naumann's voice. "Well, look here, Kevin. I'm going to stay in New York till Friday or maybe Saturday. Couple of plays in town I want to look over for maybe buying, and some people I want to see in the financial district. And I'm damned if I'll live like a bachelor here. You make it your business to find Lorayne and get her aboard a jet for New York right away. I'm staying at the Metropolitana East, and I want her here with me. Okay?"

"I'll do my best, Leo," Lyle said mechanically.

"Anything new at your end?" Naumann said.

"Not much. I'm reading a book that sounds promising so far. And I'm having lunch with Donovan on Friday about the African script. Otherwise all quiet."

"Okay. Get in touch with Lorayne. Call me back at six o'clock your time to let me know what goes."

The phone went dead.

Lyle cracked knuckle after knuckle nerv-ously. He was on the spot, now. Lorayne was — where? He didn't know. She had simply walked out, destination unknown. And Naumann had issued a regal command. He wouldn't take no for an answer. Lorayne had to he found, purely and simply.

But after he found her — then what? She wouldn't go to New York. Naumann would be furious. At her, at Lyle, at the whole universe. Heads would roll.

Lyle closed the book. His brief few hours of tranquility were ended, now. Back to confusion and hypertension.

What am I supposed to do now? he won-dered. *Ring up every hotel in Los Angeles until I find Lorayne? And then how am I going to talk Lorayne into flying east to spend the next three days snuggling up to Naumann?*

No answers.

He paced around his room for a while, stew-ing over it. The czar had issued his command. But the czar's mistress was nowhere to be found. And, as usual, it would be the czar's chamberlain who would get the axe if the czar were displeased.

Fretting, Lyle hoped for some miracle to happen. For Lorayne to call or even to come around in person to tell him that she had changed her mind and would stick with Naumann at least till the film was made. Lyle pictured the imaginary scene, Lorayne telling him of her decision, then he telling her that Naumann had summoned her to New York, Lorayne nodding, the two of them racing out to the airport to beat the departure time of the next 707. Only it wouldn't happen that way, he thought despondently. Lorayne's mind was made up. She was through with Naumann, and she was going to stay through with him, and that was that.

The minutes ticked by.

Four-fifteen, now. Four-thirty. No word from Lorayne or anybody else.

He called downstairs and said. "Did a Miss Lorayne Winant leave any messages for me at any time today?"

"Sorry, sir. No messages at all for you."

He phoned Naumann's house. Jones answered, and Lyle said, "Is Miss Winant there?"

"Sorry, sir, she is not."

"Mmm. Mr. Naumann phoned from New York. He's looking for her."

"Yes, sir, I know that," the butler said blandly.

"Did you speak to Mr. Naumann?"

"Briefly, yes sir. He told me he wanted Miss Winant to come to New York."

"That's right. Well, look, Jones. If you hear from her, tell her to call me at my hotel. Right away."

"Very good, sir. I'll tell her, sir."

Lyle hung up. No luck there. He hadn't really expected any. *Damn* Naumann!

It was ten to five, now. Five of. Five o'clock. One hour more then he had to phone Naumann back with the results of his search for Lorayne.

He fidgeted anxiously. *Why am I getting so hot and bothered?* he asked himself. *I'm an editor, not the keeper of Naumann's mistresses. It's not my responsibility to keep tabs on his women. If he was planning to stay a few days in New York, he should have taken Lorayne with him in the first place. I'm damned if I'll get an ulcer worrying about Naumann's bed companions. Lorayne isn't around. Well, tough. New York is full of girls who'd fall all over themselves to lay for Leo Naumann. He doesn't need to have Lorayne with him.*

Even the mental defiance of Naumann made him feel better. There was no reason for the state of jitters Naumann's phone call had plunged him into, none but the already wobbly state of his nerves. What happened between Naumann and Lorayne was none of his concern. He had introduced them: he couldn't be held responsible if it didn't work out.

Five-fifteen, now.

Five-thirty.

Time ticked away. Naumann would splutter, Naumann would rage — but ultimately he would come to see that it was no fault of Lyle's that Lorayne had mysteriously disappeared. At least, Lyle hoped Naumann would come to see it that way.

Quarter to six.

Ten of.

Five to six.

At six on the dot, Lyle picked up the phone and told the hotel switchboard operator, "I'd like to make a long-distance call. To New York, person-to-person collect, Mr. Leo Naumann at the Metropolitan East."

"Just one moment while I place the call for you, sir. I'll ring you back when the connection is completed."

"Okay."

He put down the phone and stared nervously at it while the minutes passed. He rehearsed the things he would say to Naumann. A simple statement of the fact: Lorayne had gone off and nobody knew where. Naumann would blow up, because he wasn't used to having his wishes frustrated. And then Lyle would have to calm him down, to soothe his ruffled feelings, to beg for forgiveness for having failed to carry out the order, to —

The phone rang.

"Mr. Lyle?" the operator said.

"Yes?"

"I've reached the Metropolitan East. They told me that your party had checked out fifteen minutes ago and was on his way to Idlewild Airport to take a plane back to Los Angeles. Do you want me to phone the airport and try to have them page Mr. Naumann there?"

Lyle clenched his jaws. Leo checked out? On his way back so soon? Why was he cutting short his visit? What had happened in the last two hours? Lyle felt a sickly, sinking feeling of impending disaster.

He said in a hoarse voice, "No, never mind that. Forget the whole thing. I'll talk to him in the morning when he gets back. Thanks anyway."

He hung up and turned away from the phone. He realized that his hands were trembling, that his body felt chilled. There was trouble ahead. He didn't know why or what kind, but he sensed it.

CHAPTER FOURTEEN

JET FLYING TIME, NON-STOP FROM New York to Los Angeles, was a little less than five hours. Leo Naumann had left for the airport shortly before six, Los Angeles time. Lyle didn't know what time his plane had left New York, but it was probably around seven — ten o'clock local time. Figure five hours in the air, and that meant Naumann would be landing in Los Angeles just around midnight.

Lyle waited up, alone in his room with a bottle of bourbon he had bought in the hotel lobby liquor store. He expected to hear from Naumann the moment the film producer set foot in the airport.

He was right.

At twenty after twelve that night, his phone rang. He pounced on it as though the building would blow up if he didn't pick up the receiver before the third ring.

"Hello?"

"I'm at the airport, Kevin. Meet me at my home in an hour. I want to talk to you."

"It's after midnight, Leo —"

"I'll expect you promptly."

Click.

Lyle cursed vividly. But Naumann hadn't left room for any choice. "Meet me at my home in an hour," Naumann had said. He had left unspoken the final words of the statement: *"or else!"*

Lyle eased himself up out of his chair, took one last nip of bourbon, and started to make himself presentable. He was, he realized, just the slightest bit tipsy. Not cockeyed drunk, the way he had been last night, but just a little bit under the influence. Just as well, he thought. Facing an angry Leo Naumann cold sober was a fate too horrible to contemplate calmly.

He stopped off in the hotel coffee shop for a cup of coffee all the same, before starting for Naumann's. It was past one by the time he eased himself into his car and turned the key. No use getting there ahead of Naumann, Lyle thought. He drove slowly, very slowly, over to Beverly Hills, turning what was usually a ten-minute drive at normal Los Angeles speeds into a twenty-minute crawl.

Naumann was there. The butler let Lyle in. Neither man exchanged a greeting. Lyle could tell from the grim expression of Jones' face that something was up.

"He's in the study," Jones said. "Go right on in." He didn't bother with his usual flurry of sirs. Lyle wondered what significance that fact had.

He entered Naumann's study.

The film producer was still dressed in his travel clothes, and they looked rumpled from the flight. He was standing near a bookcase, holding one of his riding whips in both hands. The expression on his face was more solemn than Lyle ever remembered having seen. Naumann looked more than ever like a Nazi commandment.

Lyle decided to take the cheerful approach. "Evening, Leo. Cut your trip short, I see."

"Traitor!"

"How's that again?"

Naumann looked as though he would foam at the mouth. "You didn't know where Lorayne was at four o'clock, eh? Liar! Judas!"

"Now, hold on a second, Leo —"

"Keep quiet." Naumann turned, faced him full on. "Why didn't you tell me that Lorayne came to your suite this morning after I left for New York? That she slept with you? That she told you she was leaving me?"

Lyle blinked in bewilderment. Had Naumann tapped his room somehow?

"I — well —"

"You aren't very articulate, Kevin. Suddenly you're stammering and stuttering. Did you think you could take a woman away from *me?*"

"I never intended to take anyone away from you."

"I've suspected you a long time," Naumann said coldly. "But I've never had any tangible proof. But yesterday — what was Audrey doing naked in your suite?"

The rapid-fire change of subject left Lyle groggy. "She — she came there to accuse me of conspiring to have you dump her, that was all. Because I introduced you to Lorayne.

"Why was she naked?"

"I don't know. She was drunk. Crazy, maybe. She pulled all her clothes off. Then she jumped."

"You were having an affair with her, weren't you? And with Lorayne too! Then you let me have Lorayne, knowing I'd want her for my picture — but you thought you could keep on sleeping with her when I was away!"

"No. That's not so, Leo. I told Lorayne before I took her here that I wouldn't have anything to do with her after you took her on."

Naumann glowered. "Yet she went to you this morning. Don't deny it. I have people who tell me things. Then she phoned here this afternoon to tell Jones she was moving out. What did you do to her? What did you say to her? You poisoned her mind against me!"

"Leo, I swear, I've done nothing but urge Lorayne to stay with you. If she's moving out, it's because of her own free choice. I —"

"You regretted losing her. So you turned around and asked her to leave me."

"How many times do I have to tell you —"

"Quiet!" Naumann smiled maliciously. "I insist on complete loyalty in my employees. You've done good work for me, Kevin, but perhaps I've been paying you so much that you've developed an exaggerated sense of your own importance. I must teach you to keep out of my affairs. Effective tomorrow your salary will be reduced by half. And you will report to the office five days a week. No more of this working at home. I want you where I can keep my eye on you."

"I won't let you do this to me, Leo."

"Oh? Just how will you force me to continue you at your present salary?"

"I won't. You can reduce my pay to zero, if you like. I'm quitting."

"You're *what?*"

"Resigning. Effective tonight, this minute. You can take your production company and shove it. Find someone else to read books for you. Find someone else to haggle with agents for you. Find someone else to dig up mistresses for you. I've had it. I'm through."

There was a moment of stunned silence. Naumane's tanned face turned dark, stormy. He seemed visibly fighting to find words.

He said after a moment, "You can't do it. I won't let you quit."

"Sorry, Leo. I won't let you humiliate me any more. You're an egocentric tyrant, and this is my private little revolution. I'm damned if I'll be summoned out of my room any more at midnight to be hauled on the carpet because you couldn't keep one of your own mistresses in line. I'll be damned if I'll be a party to your perverted lusts any more —"

Naumann's eyes blazed. His hand went up, and the next moment Lyle felt a stinging pain as the riding whip crashed across his face.

"Liar! Filth!" Naumann roared. "I'll crush you!"

He rushed forward, brandishing the whip. Lyle was twenty years younger than Naumann, almost a foot taller, fifty pounds heavier. And Lyle was no physical coward. But the last thing in the world that he wanted to do was get involved in a fight with Leo Naumann. Ingrained habits of respect and deference, built up over long years of association, were too strong to break. He could not lift a hand against Naumann, not even now.

The whip slashed furiously through the air. With one whick it sent a shivering line of pain up Lyle's arm; with another, it imprinted a strip of fire along his shoulders. He threw up his arms to protect himself. Naumann slapped him viciously, twice, across the mouth. Lyle felt a lip splitting, the same place where it had been cut Saturday night in the nightclub, and the warm salty taste of his own blood filled his mouth.

He tried to push Naumann away. But the little man was furious. Panting excitedly, he rained a shower of blows on Lyle, with his fists, his elbows, the whip. Lyle backed up, defending himself without striking back. He tripped suddenly over the leg of a chair and toppled backwards, landing in a heap on the floor. He looked up.

Naumann stood over him, whip high. Lyle realized numbly that Naumann was deriving an almost sexual pleasure out of administering this beating! The whip descended three more times, *whick whick whick*, once catching Lyle's left arm just below the elbow, once slicing across his shoulders, and once nipping his right cheek.

Then Naumann stepped back to survey him.

"Get up," Naumann ordered.

Lyle struggled to his feet. "I ought to break you in bits," he muttered. "You pint-sized pervert. Put that whip down and let me hit you."

"You don't have the guts to hit me," Naumann snapped. "Whip or no whip. Get out of here!"

Lyle rocked uneasily on his heels, inwardly debating making an assault on Naumann. He decided against it. The little man was in prime physical shape, and could probably inflict some serious damage. And Naumann was the sort who would fight dirty. Lyle didn't want his eyes gouged out. He didn't want a sharp-pointed shoe thudding into his groin. He didn't want a whip slashing his face to tatters.

He just wanted to get out.

"Hit me," Naumann jeered.

"I won't soil myself," Lyle said. He turned slowly, his shoulders sagging in defeat, and walked toward the door, unhurriedly, not caring whether or not Naumann sprang on him from behind and whipped him some more.

Naumann left him alone. Lyle walked silently through the long corridor toward the front door. There was no sign of the butler. Lyle opened the door for himself, stepped out, and walked slowly toward his car.

It was finished now.

No job. That, he thought, was the climax to these wild few days. He had met Lorayne on Saturday afternoon, and by Wednesday night she had managed, without really trying to, to detroy his life almost completely. He had nothing left, now. Nothing but some money in the bank and a pending divorce trial and two children who were slowly learning how not to love him any more.

He wondered what had happened between the time Naumann had called him, at four this afternoon, and the time Naumann had boarded the plane for Los Angeles.

His dazed mind tried to reconstruct a chain of events. Say, somebody at his hotel tipping off a Naumann man — probably Jones — that Naumann's new girl Lorayne had paid a visit to Lyle's room and had stayed more than an hour. Next, Lyle calling Jones, asking if he had heard from Lorayne, further arousing the butler's suspicions. Finally, Lorayne calling Jones and — perhaps drunkenly — announcing that she was not going to keep on living with Naumann.

So then Jones might have placed a call to Naumann, in New York, telling him that Lorayne was pulling out on him and that Lyle was somehow involved. And, on the spur of the moment, his empire threatened, Naumann made arrangements to rush back to Los Angeles and bring the errant vassal to heel immediately.

Consider me brought to heel, Lyle thought.

He speculated as to whether Naumann had

really intended to maneuver him into quitting, or had just expected to humiliate him by cutting his pay. Probably the former. Naumann couldn't seriously have expected Lyle to meekly accept the stinging blow of a $25,000 a year pay cut. It was an open invitation for a resignation, though Lyle was surprised that he had found the courage to break loose.

Now what, old man?

He didn't know. He was very tired. His shirt was torn, his face was bleeding, his body ached miserably where Naumann had struck him. But he didn't want to go back to the hotel. He didn't want to walk into the lobby looking like something found in an alleyway.

But where could he go?

He let the car take him. It rolled along almost of its own accord and came to a stop in front of a bar. The same bar, he realized, that he had been in last night. The clip-joint with the B-girls.

What the hell. At least it's familiar territory.

He walked in.

The same waiter was on duty. He looked at Lyle quizzically, then managed a quick smile.

"Good evening, sir."

"Hello. Got a free table?"

"Sure." He was led to a booth in back, perhaps the same one he had occupied the night before. The waiter studiously ignored Lyle's cuts and bruises as he said, "Will it be martinis again, sir?"

Lyle nodded. "And there's that girl who

works here. Jeanie. Send her over."

She came to his table quickly, a glassy smile fixed on her face. She was dressed the same way as the night before, a loose blouse hanging open, no bra underneath. When she saw him she called out, "Hey Jimmy, you came back, huh?"

"Sit down, Jeanie. Have a drink on me. Have a couple, matter of fact."

She signalled to the waiter. A martini arrived for him, a rye-and-ginger for her.

"Jeez, Jimmy," she said. "You been in a fight or something? You're all cut up."

"I walked into a fan," Lyle said.

"Gotta watch out for that sort of stuff."

"I'm careless sometimes."

The martini disappeared into him. So did the second and the third. Jeanie matched him drink for drink, keeping up a steady line of moronic chatter. When the third drinks came, Lyle reached out and grabbed her glass before she could pick it up. He took a sip and grinned knowingly at her.

"There's no liquor in here. It's just straight ginger ale, isn't it?"

She tried to fake it. "You're kidding. Let's see." She put it to her lips. "Uh-uh, Jimmy. This thing has an ounce of rye in it."

"I tasted it. It's just ginger ale."

She shook her head. "You've had too much gin, that's all. Your taste buds ain't working right any more."

Lyle chuckled. "That won't wash, Jeanie. It's all phony, isn't it? But don't think I let that

bother me. What does matter, anyhow? Everything's phony. I want to buy you drinks. It's the
gesture that counts, not the reality. It's all the
same to me whether that glass of yours is full of
booze or full of ginger ale. Just so long as I keep
on thinking it's got real liquor in it. So I do. I
think it has real liquor in it."

"You talk a little crazy sometimes, Jimmy."

"I feel a little crazy sometimes." He polished
off his third martini and looked around unsteadily. "Let's go into that back room of yours."

"Sure, Jimmy. Sure. But you got to settle
your check first. That's the rule."

"How much is it?"

"I'll get the waiter."

"Never mind," he said. He took six dollars
out of his wallet. "That ought to cover it, the tip
and everything. Six drinks, six dollars. It sounds
right. Okay?"

"I suppose. Come on."

She helped him up. He was very shaky on
his pins, now. She led him further back through
the cocktail lounge, then through a door in the
rear. They passed through a corridor with wash-
rooms to the right and left, and entered a little
room at the end of the hall. Just a cubicle, win-
dowless, with the stale smell of sweat hanging
in the air. It contained a narrow cot with a sagging mattress, a sink, a toilet bowl, and a hat-
rack with some hangers on it. Lyle stepped
woozily inside. Jeanie closed the door and
pushed a little bolt home.

"How cozy," he said.

"It's okay. You got to pay me now. That's the rule around here."

"Sure. How much?"

"Ten," she said. She hesitated, then added, possibly improvising, "plus five bucks special fee. Makes fifteen bucks altogether."

"Absolutely." He took out his wallet again and thumbed through the bills. Once again that thousand-dollar bill of Naumann't peered up at him. The damned bill was haunting him. He hadn't taken it to the bank yet. He thumbed past it, found a ten and a five, handed them to the girl. She put the money away quickly and began to unbutton her blouse.

Her breasts were big and heavy, slightly cowlike and beginning to develop a sag. The aureoles were huge, as big as silver dollars, and the nipples stuck up like sentinels. Lyle watched detachedly as she stepped out of her skirt and pulled her panties down, keeping her stockings on. She was a big woman, with a round belly and thick thighs. She lay down on the cot, as Lyle removed his clothes to join her.

"Hold it," she said. She reached out, picked up a flat metal box that was lying on the side of the bed. "Here. Use this."

He looked at it oddly, a drunken smile on his face. She helped him with it. Then she pulled him down to her.

He felt no particular desire, but his body acted for him, and he went to her. She gave out a counterfeit groan of passion. He felt sick. After making love to women like Donna, like Audrey, like — especially — Lorayne, it was a horrid travesty to lie on top of this plump drab girl and perform the same act. But he went through with it. She put up a good show, sighing and whim-pering when he held her fleshy breasts. Her body went tight against him and she began to move in a series of little quick motions, and in a joyless and pleasureless way he felt himself re-sponding . . .

She started to dress again as he adjusted his tie. He looked at her, and there was a coppery taste in his mouth, and his body ached pecu-liarly as though he had not really achieved sat-isfaction at all.

"Do me a favor, Jeanie?"

"What?"

"Go outside and get me a drink. A martini. I'll sit right here. I'm not feeling so good." He handed her a dollar. "Go on. Bring it back here. Keep the change for yourself."

She was gone about five minutes. He sat quite still, his brain disconnected. Then she was back, and handing him a drink, and he took it with shaking hands and gulped it own like needed medicine.

"Come on, now. Let's go back outside and you can have all the drinks you like out there."

He let her lead him back into the bar. The world was very hazy, now. He remembered hav-ing another drink, then going back to the wash-room, then having still another drink. Jeanie had left him for another client. He sat nursing the cocktail — his sixth of the evening? Seventh? and getting drowsier and drowsier.

His head drooped forward.

Sooooo tired . . . .

The scene with Naumann was only a dim memory now. Donna, Lorayne, the children, just figures out of a misty past.

"Another drink," he muttered.

He was out cold before it arrived.

CHAPTER FIFTEEN

AND THEN HE WAS WAKING UP. He was cold, very cold, and he opened his one eye and saw pavement an inch away, and knew that he was lying on his belly in some back alley. He ached all over, and he felt sick to his stomach and wanted to throw up. He remained still for what seemed like hours, gathering the strength to get up.

He looked around, still lying on the pavement. He saw something brown lying near him. He reached for it.

His wallet.

He looked at it, opened the flap where he kept his money. Empty. He began to laugh hollowly. Drunk and dumped in an alley and robbed. Naumann's thousand dollars was gone, and so was a couple of hundred that he had been carrying around as well.

For some reason, they had left him his wristwatch. He looked at it, and with an effort read the time: ten past seven. It was a chilly morning, with a hint of rain in the sky. Lyle gingerly touched his skull. No bruises. He hadn't been blackjacked. He had simply passed out and had been efficiently relieved of his money.

A damned shame, he thought. He needed the money, now — now that he had no job. *But nobody's fault but my own,* he told himself. He struggled to get up, didn't quite make it, and sat down heavily. A dirty white cat crept out from behind a nearby garbage can and stared at him with cold contempt for a long moment. then padded silently off into the morning. Lyle closed his eyes an instant, took a deep breath, rose first to one knee and then to a standing position.

Easy now. Don't fall on your rear again.

He tottered, wobbled, and held up. Looking around, he saw that he was in an alley behind the cocktail lounge. At this hour of the morning, the place was shut tight. The whole neighborhood was silent as a tomb. Unsteadily, Lyle moved up the alley toward the front of the building. His head was splitting. He felt filthy, bruised, hung over. Cloudy memories of the night before stirred in his mind. The quarrel with Naumann. Coming here. Getting drunk. Lying on a stinking cot with a B-girl, holding one jiggly breast in each hand. Passing out. Waking up.

So this is what absolute bottom feels like, he thought. *You lose your wife to another man, you lose your mistress even, you lose your job, and then you wake up robbed in an alley and find that you've even lost your self-respect. Your own existence nauseates you. You start feeling like a character in an existentialist novel.*

He emerged out front. Miraculously, the car was still there, untouched. He fumbled in his pocket and found the key. Whoever had robbed him had only been interested in cash, it seemed. Not that they had done badly just on the money in his wallet.

He got into the car, leaned forward, rested his forehead on the steering wheel for a while. When he felt stronger, he started the car and, making a ragged U-turn, headed back toward the hotel.

At half past seven in the morning, the hotel was quiet. The desk clerk looked at him briefly as he came in, frowned at his battered and dirty appearance, and looked away again. The elevator operator maintained a dignified superciliousness as he took Lyle up.

Once inside his suite, he looked at himself in the mirror.

My God, what a mess.

He looked like he'd been crawling in a coalbin. His white shirt was filthy and ripped in half a dozen places. His lower lip was puffed. There was a smear of soot across his forehead, and cuts on both his cheeks. His hair was matted and tangled. His eyes were the eyes of a madman. He looked as though he had aged ten years overnight.

He realized he was trembling. He peeled off

his clothing, wincing at the cuts and bruises, and went into the bathroom, carefully swabbing himself clean. He moved with precise, mechanical gestures, deliberately forcing himself not to think about his situation.

When he had tidied up, he picked up the phone and called Ben Montereale's home number. The lawyer would be having breakfast about this time, Lyle figured.

The lawyer's wife answered the phone. In a low voice Lyle introduced himself and asked to speak to Ben. A moment later, Montereale said, "What is it, Kevin?"

"I need to see you, Ben."

"I'll be at the office after nine."

"No — could you come here?" Lyle asked, in a whisper.

"Speak up. I can hardly hear you."

"Come here. To the hotel. I — I can't go out. I was beaten up last night. And robbed. I woke up in an alley this morning. I got rolled for better than thirteen hundred dollars."

"Jesus Christ," Montereale muttered. "You must take trouble pills or something."

"That isn't the half of it. Naumann fired me last night. Or I quit. Same thing. I was put in a position where I couldn't do anything else but walk out. Ben, I'm starting to think of killing myself. Everything's closing in on me all at once."

Montereale muttered something beneath his breath that sounded like a curse. Then he said, "Stop talking like an idiot. Look here, I've got a

very important conference at my office at half
past nine. It ought to break around half past
ten, and I'll come right over to your place by
eleven at the latest."

"Can't you come here first?"

"You're acting babyish. Snap out of it, Kevin!
I hope to have some good news for you, anyway."

"That'll be a novelty."

"So forget this crap about killing yourself.
You don't even begin to know how tough things
can get. Just hold tight till I get there. Have you
called in the cops on this robbery bit?"

"No. Not yet."

"Hold off, then. They can't do anything for
you, more likely than not, and you don't want to
keep popping up in hot water. How'd you get
robbed?"

"I went out for some drinks after seeing
Naumann. I had one too many, caved in, and
woke up in the back alley. I could give you the
name of the place —"

"That won't do any good. They'll just say that
when you conked out they put you out in the
street. They aren't responsible for the contents
of your pockets. Look, Kevin, I can't gab any
longer. I'll come over around eleven, okay? And
you can tell me what happened between you and
Naumann."

"Around eleven. Okay," Lyle said tiredly, and
hung up.

There was a soft knock at the door.

He looked up. "Who's there?"

A very small voice answered, "Lorayne."

209

His heart began to race furiously. Rising, he went to the door, opened it.

Lorayne gasped. "Kevin! What happened to you?"

"Plenty," he said. "What brings you here?"

"I had to see you," she said. "I didn't wake you up, did you? I wanted to get here before you left for the office, because I can't go there."

He shook his head bitterly. "You didn't wake me, no. And I'm not going to the office today."

"I wasn't able to sleep last night," Lorayne said. She looked pale, tense, anguished. "I got a room, you know. At the Normandie, three blocks from here. And I've been pacing around since yesterday afternoon. Kevin, I don't know what to do. I'm so mixed up about everything."

"In what way?"

"I love you so goddamned much," she whispered. "And when you sent me packing out of here yesterday I felt like jumping into the ocean. I know, I'm a nuisance. I'm plaguing you, and you've got other things on your mind. But — but can't we work something out? I'm thinking of packing up, clearing out of Hollywood altogether. Going to New York, maybe, trying to get into television work there or something. Anything to get out of this horrid city. But if you'd only give me a word — just a maybe that after the divorce —"

She stopped. He moistened his lips and said carefully, "Honestly, Lorayne, I don't know if I'm coming or going any more. I can't predict the future as far as tomorrow morning. let alone beyond the divorce. For one thing, I'm out of a job. Naumann fired me last night."

"He *what?*"

Quickly, Lyle summed up the sequence of events for her. Lorayne listened, pale, wide-eyed.

When he finished she said, "Oh, I'm sorry. Kevin. So terribly sorry. It's all my fault, isn't it?"

"Mine as much an anybody's"

"No," she insisted. "If I hadn't walked out on Leo, he never would have gotten angry at you. None of this would have happened if I'd listened to you and tried to make a go of it with Leo. But I had to be stubborn. And now I'm back in no-wheresville, and I've dragged you there with me."

"Lorayne —"

But she had turned away and was sobbing quietly. He watched her uncomfortably for a moment; sobbing women always left him ill at ease. Then he walked over to her and rested the tips of his fingers lightly on her shoulders. She didn't look at him. In a tomblike voice she said, "We've made a fine mess of things, haven't we, Kevin?"

He didn't answer. He felt tired, and lonely, and suddenly very old. He dug his hands deeper into her yielding flesh. Abruptly she spun around and she was kissing him, savagely, her breasts boring into him, her body grinding against his, her tongue deep within his mouth.

They remained that way a long moment, as

though afraid to release each other for fear new troubles would strike them. Convulsively, Lorayne quivered and sobbed. He ran his hand down her back, cupped his fingers over the resilience of her slacks-clad buttocks.

There was a knock at the door.

Guiltily, Lyle and Lorayne sprang apart. Lorayne looked at him uncertainly and said, "What should I do?"

"Wait. Who's there?" he called, more loudly.

"Ben."

Lyle frowned, glanced at Lorayne, and whispered. "He's my lawyer. He doesn't bite." To the door, he called, "I'm coming," and opened it.

Montereale stepped in, his familiar portfolio under one arm, and looked a trifle puzzledly at Lorayne. Quickly, Lyle said, "Ben Montereale, Miss Lorayne Winant. We both used to be with Leo Naumann. She came to see me about half an hour ago."

Montereale shrugged, his private form of salutation. "Pleased to meet you, Miss Winant" Then, with a sharp look at Lyle, he said, "I think we'd better talk privately, Lyle. If Miss Winant will excuse us —"

"Wait in the lobby," Lyle told her. "I want to talk to you again after I'm through with Ben."

Lorayne left without protest. The moment she was gone, Montereale said, "She's the one you've been sleeping with?"

"We saw each other this past weekend. There's nothing between us right now. It's a complicated story, Ben."

212

"I'll bet. Well, that's a sweet bit, anyway. You always did have good taste in women, Kevin." Montereale's deep-set little eyes bored diamond-like into him. "But for a grown man you act like a damned fool sometimes."

"Just lately. It seems that everything I've done lately has gone sour."

"You're really out of work, are you?"

"I wasn't making it up."

"Got any prospects for another job?"

Lyle shrugged. "I haven't given it much thought yet. I suppose I can find one, unless Naumann puts the pressure on to keep me blacklisted. At the very worst I can go back to writing scripts. Grade Q monster movies at $500 a week. *Ogzog, Thing from Outer Space.* Enough people are in debted to me so that I'll get along."

"I'm glad to hear that," Montereale said. "Because you're going to owe me one hell of a pile of money by the time this case is finished. Aside from my regular fee, there's now the matter of $1500 for a private detective."

"Fifteen hun —"

"And worth every penny of it," Montereale said with a sly smile. "I put him on Donna about two weeks ago. He watched her night and day. Had a very interesting report to turn in, too. You jackass, don't you have more sense than to go lay that woman when she's trying to steal your kids?"

Color flamed in Lyle's battered face. "You mean he —"

"He watched the whole thing through a window, night before last. Good thing I had given him a picture of you, or there would have been a real mess. Christ almighty, Lyle, you seem to do everything the opposite from what I tell you to do. I say keep away from women, you go out chasing quail. I say be careful about Donna, so you let her lay you. I say stay out of trouble, and you get yourself rolled in an alley, you have a crazy girl jump out your window —"

Lyle shook his head. "It's just been a streak of lousy luck, that's all. I haven't been able to get myself untangled. I go from one foulup to another." He looked down at the floor dispiritedly. "I suppose all this is a prelude to telling me that you're dropping the case and want to be paid off. Well, I can't say I blame you."

"I'm not dropping the case. We've won it."

"Eh?"

Montereale grinned broadly. "I shudder for your children, Kevin. With two nitwits like you and Donna for parents, they'll have the lousiest endowment of common sense any two people ever had. Donna's just as dumb as you are."

"What are you sayng?"

"I'm saying that she managed to snatch defeat out of the jaws of victory. She made a fatal slip. I got her right where it hurts." With a cat-that-has-just-bobbled-up-the-canary smile, he picked up his portfolio and drew out two large, glossy black-and-white prints.

Lyle gasped.

The first print showed two people in bed. The

furniture was unmistakably that of Donna's bedroom. Donna was lying on top of the sheets, looking up in astonishment at the camera. Her legs were parted, and there was a man with her, his head turned so that half his face was exposed to the camera. He was Bruce Caldwell. It was obvious that they had been interrupted while making love. That much was anatomically clear.

The second picture showed Caldwell and Donna off the bed and racing toward the cameraman. Both of them were stark naked and dumbstruck with surprise and anger. Donna's nostrils were spread like an animal's: Caldwell was photographed in a state of arousal, shaking a fist furiously at the camera.

Lyle stared at first one picture, then the second. Both of them masterpieces that would fetch a good price from any connoisseur.

In a low voice he said, "When were these taken?"

"Last night, around midnight. That detective was worth every penny he charged. Donna got overconfident. She figured she had you over a barrel, and she could take some risks herself. Around eleven-thirty Caldwell showed up at the house. My man let himself in and burst into the bedroom. Took two shots and scrammed. He called me late last night, after they were developed. I phoned you here around two in the morning, but nobody answered."

"And — and how are you going to use these?"

"I already have," Montereale said with a

grin. "I asked Donna's lawyer to pay me a visit this morning, and I showed him the pictures. He threw in the towel. He knows when he's licked. Donna doesn't stand a chance of winning the case, now. The best she can hope for is a long bloody squabble that'll tarnish both your reputations and hurt the kids tremendously. So we've worked out a tentative settlement. You'll divorce her quietly on the grounds of adultery, using the pictures, and she won't contest. There'll be a fifty-fifty division of assets. But you get the house and the kids. She'll have the right to visit them weekends a year and to have them live with her ten days a year. Since she plans to remarry right away, there's no alimony problem. It means she gets away with most of your cash assets, but there was no helping that."

Lyle looked dazed. "Everything is happening so gaddam fast!"

"That's the way I work, Kevin. I bide my time and then I smash down hard. My only worry was that you'd bollix things up beyond repair before I could make my move." Montereale rose. "You can keep those prints as souvenirs, if you like. I've got plenty more."

Lyle shook his head. "No thanks. I can get along without ever seeing these prints again. They turn my stomach."

Montereale put them back in his portfolio and walked toward the door. "There'll be another meeting tomorrow to get things worked out finally. After that it's just a matter of getting the decree. And paying the bills." Montereale grinned. "So long, Kevin."

"Yeah. And thanks. And — say, Ben —"

"What?"

"On your way out, in the lobby — tell Miss Winant to come upstairs."

"Sure," Montereale said, with a wink.

He left. Lorayne entered a few minutes later. "Well?" she said.

"Things are progressing," he told her, concealing his joy. "He's a good lawyer."

"So I've heard." Lorayne walked over to the table on which Lyle had spread out the contents of his wallet. She picked up the photos of Jeff and Rhona. "Are these your children?"

"Yes."

"They're beautiful children. Such wonderful smiles. They don't deserve the misery they're going through."

"Maybe things will be better for them soon." He could contain the news no longer. It bubbled out of him, now, everything Montereale had said.

Tears glistened in Lorayne's eyes. "Oh, Kevin — I'm so happy for you. At last something is working out well for you."

He smiled. "I feel ten years younger already. After breakfast I've got to start calling people up. Looking for jobs. Decent jobs, not Leo Naumann-type jobs. And I'll have to start asking about getting you some screen tests, too." He hesitated a moment. "Unless you want to forget about the movies and just stay home and have babies."

"Unless — babies —" Lorayne blinked diz‐ zily. "Are you saying —"

"I'm saying I love you," he grinned. He stepped across the room, took her in his arms. Her breasts rose to his touch, firm and warm. She quivered in his arms, clung tight to him, made throaty little love‐sounds. Lyle closed his eyes. He had been through a few days of hell, but it was all ending now. Time to make new beginnings. He was free of Donna, free of Leo Naumann, free of all the clinging bonds of the past. There was only Lorayne — and a whole long lifetime ahead.

THE END

TO THE READER

If you enjoyed this book, you will be glad to know that there are many others just as well written, just as interesting, to be had in the Fiction House Press Library.

You will find the Fiction House Press Library online at

www.FictionHousePress.com

www.ingramcontent.com/pod-product-compliance
Lightning Source LLC
Chambersburg PA
CBHW031109260626

47172CB00001B/283